THE PRESIDENT SHOP

DESING & LAYOUT Nikša Eršek
PUBLISHED BY Sandorf Passage
South Portland, Maine, United States
IMPRINT OF Sandorf
Severinska 30, Zagreb, Croatia
sandorf.hr | contact@sandorf.hr
PRINTED BY Tiskara Zrinski, Čakovec

Sandorf Passage books are available to the trade through Independent Publishers Group: ipgbook.com | (800) 888-4741.

Library of Congress Control Number: 2020944409

National and University Library Zagreb Control Number: 001077020

ISBN: 978-9-53351-295-2

sandorfpassage.org

THE PRESIDENT SHOP

VESNA MARIC

SAN-
DORF
PAS-
SAGE

SOUTH PORTLAND | MAINE

for Elena

Chapter 1

ROSA PUSHED MONA into the world on a December evening. And as the infant emerged from the soft, pink chamber of the womb at 7:13pm, under the luminous neon line of light on the ceiling, it was his countenance that Mona saw first: the President, as rendered in a black-and-white portrait in an ornately flowery gilded frame. It was as if the picture, or the picture frame, was the President's cell, and his figure the cell's silent nucleus, floating around the country's interiors, watching all. The President was handsome, with high cheekbones that held his face taut like pegs pull a tent or wind yanks a flag. Mostly the pictures of him were black and white, from his youth. Later, when Mona was nearing the first decade of her life, firm on her legs and lean in her body, the pictures of the President were in color, his aged countenance now full, sporting dark sunglasses, liver spots, and a military cap. Often, in his autumn years, a Cuban cigar poked stiffly from between his canines.

The doctor rushed in, perspiring and smelling of cigarettes and alcohol. He had been drinking and smoking in a bar moments before being summoned by the panicked Diogen, Ruben's younger brother, who had been helping Rosa in the shop.

Rosa's waters broke across the floor like in the movies, propelling her into the fastest labor known to womankind, as if Mona insisted she be born right there in the President Shop.

The doctor, Gypsy songs still pounding in his head, arrived at the shop and found Rosa stretched out across the floor on top of the national flag, the five-pointed star beneath her. The baby was delivered upon it, curled like a wreath. The red star crowned her like an aura, a celestial body around the newborn, delivered from the heavens. Rosa was swollen and red and the many globes of her body—the belly a vast sun behind which nestled the aureole of the breasts—radiated like circular echoes. Tears ran down Rosa's face. She looked down at the baby and smiled with her beautiful mouth. The umbilical cord pulsated between them.

Thereafter, whenever they saw the doctor in the street Rosa would say to Mona "This is the man who birthed you," as if only the doctor had been the one to do the work of labor. The doctor always smelled of alcohol and cigarettes, and glimmered with sweat, like a silver birch in the wind.

Chapter 2

MONA COULD NOT have taken in the details of the President Shop on the day of her birth but if she had, she would have seen a display of the President's portrait from all sides. Profile, semi-profile, front facing; young, middle-aged, old; wartime, post war; military clothing—fatigues and dress uniforms—and crisp civilian suits. There were pictures of the President driving one of his limousines in a white suit, decorated with military honors, his hands gloved in white silk; the President's wife beside him, wearing a bouffant hairstyle like a dark medieval crown.

But Mona, her newborn soul still mindless and full of stars, grasped that birth was suffering and love, and that the outside world was filled with odors and sensations she could not resist or pull away from. She discovered that she could cry, and that most of the time, if she cried, she would be filled with sweet breast milk and embraced by Rosa into a softness and fluidity that closed around her like tulip petals.

People came to see Mona. They put their faces into the cot, made noises. The first people, the ones whose sounds she recognized, their voices vibrating to her through the walls of the womb months before, were those of Rosa, Ruben, Diogen, and, of course, the President. Ruben was a boom. Her father's voice made the air shake, but when he held Mona he trembled with tenderness. Diogen always sang. Rosa spoke softly and laughed like a storm. When Ruben spoke of the President his voice became something of a whisper. The newborn Mona could fit inside the palm of his hand, and sometimes he carried her around like a loaf of bread, to soothe her wailing.

The President's voice mostly came from the radio or off a vinyl record, when Ruben would play one of the President's speeches. He had a clipped way of speaking, a soft accent, and sometimes he made jokes that made Ruben and Rosa laugh. But mostly he was serious. "What are the phenomena of nationalism? Here are some of them. One. National egoism, from which many other negative traits of nationalism are derived, as for example—a desire for foreign conquest, a desire to oppress other nations, a desire to impose economic exploitation upon other nations, and so on."

"Yes!" Ruben would shout. "That's right!"

"Two. National chauvinism, which is also a source of many other negative traits of nationalism, as for example national hatred, the disparagement of other nations, the disparagement of their history, culture, and scientific activities and scientific achievements, and so on, the glorification of developments in their own history that were negative and which from our Marxist point of view is considered negative."

"Exactly, said Ruben. "That's exactly right. Who can think that is not right? You don't even have to be a Marxist to find that is the way things are."

Diogen said nothing. Rosa nodded as she wiped the dust off the President's many busts, cast in copper, silver, bronze and kept in various glass cases in the shop. But there was a single one in gold, locked up in a shatterproof glass cabinet. This was the pride and joy of the President Shop.

Chapter 3

THE LOCKED UP shatterproof, fireproof glass cabinet was purchased abroad and manufactured to protect expensive artwork. The state had offered Ruben half of the money to acquire it and protect the bust; the bust, apart from being gold, was made by the country's most renowned sculptor. There was no possibility of putting a price on its immense value, which was both material and sentimental, for the Nation and for Ruben. The bust was not for sale; Ruben was its steward. The Nation had rewarded him and Rosa with this gesture, for their service to the country as Partisans, and the hard work they'd been doing for decades, promoting and keeping alive the President's work and image, after Ruben had injured his back once and for all, lifting the heavy tools in the factory, where he had worked as a machinist.

The President Shop was wood paneled, honey-colored and light poured in through large windows. The long counter had a glass top; beneath sat pins and badges adorned with the President's signature and various interpretations of his likeness. There were miniature flags of the Nation, flecked with small red stars. Customers came in, purchased them, and stuck them into the lapels of their jackets, or pierced the sides of their hats.

Women pinned their silk scarves with them. Ruben explained to his customers how the President signed in Cyrillic in order to show that both the Latin and Cyrillic alphabet belonged to the Nation's people, that he loved both with equal merit. "Our people must always stick together," Ruben would never fail to add. But most people came in to take a look at the gold bust. It sat behind the counter and most of the time was covered with a cloth the color of moss. Mona often thought it was as if the bust was a secret, set deep in the north of the woods of the shop, a mysterious, radiating spot.

In the afternoons, the hot ball of the sun bounced against the windows and landed inside the shop, turning the apples in the bowl into globes of gold. The afternoons were when Ruben used to pick up one of his books and read out important quotations. Rosa and Mona knew that this was the time to be quiet and listen.

Ruben would cough and enunciate as he read from *The Art of Being* by Erich Fromm: "If the blue-and white-collar workers in an industrial enterprise or the nurses and employees in the hospital once they cease to be 'employed' participated in managing the institutions by themselves, if they could build a community together with all who work in the same institution, they would have a task set before them that can achieve excellence and the rationality of organization and the quality of human relations. In such productive work each would also work productively on his own life. Aside from the place of work as a social organization, the optimal organization of society as a whole gives everyone the possibility to contribute with his whole heart. However, to achieve this would require that society and its political representative, the state, ceased to be powers that stood over and against the citizen, but that they are the product of his work. At the present stage of alienation this is quite impossible; in a humanized society, aside from his own life, society itself becomes man's most important work fact—and the ends of both coincide."

If Diogen happened to come by at this time, he would invariably turn away when he saw Ruben with the book, or go in the back and bang the dishes, and Ruben would look toward the door with irritation.

Rosa was in charge of the shop's appearance for the most part, but it was Ruben who would often stay behind and clean the special protective box with a special cloth. When the shop closed and the blinds crashed down, Ruben would open the case with the key that hung on a golden chain around his neck. When he took out the bust it weighed down his hand beautifully. He'd run his fingers over the sculptor's shapes and strokes; he'd put his soft fingertips inside the golden President's eyes, run them across the cheekbones, across the neck and down the shoulders. It was a small bust; the President's head fit inside Ruben's palm. He'd clean it with a velvet cloth, making sure every crevice was covered.

At night, when the shop and the town were purring under the inky caresses of darkness, and when there was the possibility of oblivion, as well as restless remembrance, Ruben would carry the golden bust, inside its case, down to the fallout shelter. The President had ordered that fallout shelters be planned within the structure of all new buildings and apartment blocks, and that old buildings have their storage basements fortified in case of a nuclear attack, which for a time, and if one were to trust the news, seemed imminent. The Nation had to be ready for any type of attack, especially for nuclear war, and the citizens, including women, had to go on monthly emergency exercises. So, Ruben reasoned, although unlikely right now, while the slow-paced town they inhabited was in the depths of its sleep, one never knew where danger might come from, and if nuclear warfare were to erupt all of a sudden, it would be immoral of him to take care of the gold bust first, before his wife and child and brother, of course. They would be his priority, but he could also never forgive himself if something were to happen to the bust, if it were stolen—God forbid—or worse, became radioactive so that no one could touch it and dust would gather on it and Ruben would have to hand it over to the authorities, who would then prod it with those measuring sticks that tell you how toxic any individual thing is, and they'd keep it under observation, this beautiful statue, possibly never give it back. That wouldn't do. Ruben wouldn't survive such an injustice, so he did what he thought was best, and he carried the box and the statue, which must have weighed as much as a small child, he carried them downstairs, into the shelter, and deposited them in the safe box inside the shelter, to which only Ruben and Rosa knew the code. And in the morning, when the President's golden head and the hot ball of the sun looked as if they belonged to kindred tribes, Ruben would carry it back up to the shop.

Chapter 4

THE STORIES OF the President's childhood and early life were known to all throughout the Nation. Mona particularly liked them. The President was born poor in a small village in the north of the country, the eldest of five children, all of them barely educated. He was always smart, prudent, hard working, and had a love of—and a longing for—fine clothes. He narrated his life stories to the Nation, via books and speeches. He told of his strict, yet gentle and loving, mother, who had to ration food for her children, locking up the daily bread in the larder, the occasion of a visit from unexpected guests an opportunity for the children to ask her for a piece, for she could not refuse them bread in front of others, her pride would not allow it; but after the guests left, the children were scolded for their brazenness. Mona's favorite story was that of the President being left in charge of his siblings, while his parents were off at a multi-day wedding celebration. Spurred on by a mean old aunt, who had assured him his parents, full from the wedding food, would not mind if he boiled up a piece of the pig's head that had been left aside by his mother for feasts and family celebrations, the boy did just that. His siblings were very hungry. He went in the larder; the pig's head sat on the shelf, eyes closed as if in prayer. The President sawed off a piece from the neck, boiled it up for a soup, which gave them all a terrible stomachache—the fat was too strong for them. Upon his parents' return, the little President incurred his mother's disapproval. Yet his mother did not punish him, for she could tell the difference between the boy's gullibility and her sister's vexing meddling. The President ruled over the Nation, Mona thought, the same way his mother had ruled over her children—with a firm yet fair hand. He rationed the Nation's goods with prudence and wisdom, and if someone did err, the President acted justly, thought Mona. Everyone also knew the story of the President's adolescent apprenticeship as a locksmith, and his wandering around from one mentor to another, where he learned the skills of a machinist, fixing various engines and agricultural machines, walking to Trieste in search of work, and returning home, empty-handed; this is how he also learned his most useful skill of all—that of survival.

Mona was fascinated by the origin and shaping of the President's revolutionary character through his service in the Austro-Hungarian Army; the country that was not yet the Nation was part of that glamorous and expansive empire at the time. Having gone to work in Germany and Austria for various automobile factories, where he had already been involved with workers' unions, earning himself a reputation as a socialist agitator, the President was drafted into military service, and since he found himself feeling lonely amid foreigners, he applied for a transfer to a town near his family home. This he achieved, but soon regretted. Upon arriving at his new station with his blond mane intact—since the Austrians had not deemed it necessary that new soldiers' heads be shaven—a local commander with a panache for sadism took a shaver to the President's head and made a cross in his locks, thus humiliating the President and making him regret his decision to transfer; his hair was thoroughly shaved off thereafter. The young man, who was a keen and skilful fencer, also won various fencing competitions. Yet his dexterity was met with disapproval by the commanders, who did not like seeing a peasant boy excel at anything above his station. Thus the President learned that humiliation was inherent inside hierarchical systems.

World War I broke out while the President was in the army. He wished to surrender himself to the Bolshevik Russians, but found that difficult, since the local police arrested him on various occasions; his political views were becoming more widely known. Despite this, wherever he went, the President took up with the local workers, organizing them into unions and helping the peasants. Through various military operations and wartime arrests, the President ended up in Siberia, as a prisoner of war. He escaped and hid for several months in Kazakh villages, working as a machinist and living inside caves, keeping up with the progress of the Bolsheviks through meetings with local workers. He illegally boarded trains in attempts to escape, was arrested again, spent weeks in rat-infested cells, was sick to the point of dying, shared meager food with his fellow prisoners, until he finally reached the borders of his country again. Throughout this time, he learned that he hated war and that the spirit of the revolution had to be strengthened at all costs, and that the upper class was exploiting the workers for its own gains and for the preservation of its wealth, and that this had to stop. During his time in Russia, he had also managed to marry and have a son, all by the age of twenty-two. Mona had cut out a picture of the President's first wife and little son, and kept it pinned to her bedroom wall.

Upon returning to his native land, the President took to organizing the Communist Party, and trying to bridge the various factions that appeared amongst the unions, and he emerged as the strongest candidate for a unified party leader. He worked as a machinist again, at shipbuilding yards in various parts of the country, but was always fired because of his revolutionary activities. He was again persecuted and arrested, and again he escaped prison—once by way of filing down the iron cell bars and breaking them, like in the old cartoons—but then was arrested once more and served a six-year sentence in the decade preceding World War II. Upon his arrest, the President did not want to deny being a communist, even though the Communist party had been declared illegal. "Why should I denounce such a strong idea, one that I believed in and for which I was ready to give my life?" he said in his later retellings of his biography. In prison, he was tortured and he went on a hunger strike, and even the President's first wife was arrested. All this had been told to a series of writers once the Nation was formed, and published in various collected volumes that most people inside the country had on their bookshelves. The Maric family of course had several collections, and, sometimes after dinner, Ruben read aloud from the books to Mona and to snoozing Rosa.

The President spoke of prison as a formative experience, full of activists and workers and intellectuals, all of whom managed to create a kind of a school for a communist education. The inmates fought to be kept in one room, rather than in solitary confinement, where they were being kept originally. They won this right through hunger strikes that left the authorities with no choice but to relent. They studied Marxism in depth, and got local criminals to bring them books in exchange for cigarettes. An entire library was created, but books had to be camouflaged. A Marxist text had pages from *The Count of Monte Cristo* added to them, the President said, so that the guards would not suspect anything. "Anyway, even if the guard had looked properly at the pages where Marx discusses economic issues, he'd have thought a Count Monte Cristo had written them!" said the President, and Mona, Ruben, and Rosa chuckled.

The President spoke of the fact that, inside their cell, everyone had to study a topic and teach it to the rest of the inmates; everyone in the cell was, in his words, "a bit of a clever clogs, so it was hard to teach." And it had fallen upon him to give a lecture on the topic of cosmogony, and here, he said, "I got pretty mixed up. The topic was too tough to understand!" He also learned languages in prison, including English and Esperanto. In 1934, he was released and became a member of the Central Communist Party.

The President was soft, jolly, wise, practical, tough, fair, focused, and, frequently, funny. Mona admired the President's determination and his sense of fairness and loyalty—he never betrayed his comrades, even when tortured—and she loved his sense of humor. Ruben thought these were the qualities that any person of quality, so to speak, had to possess or work toward possessing. It was part of his problem with Diogen. Diogen did not hold those traits—or the stories—in great esteem. He had tried to get Diogen to listen to the President's stories, or at least to read them.

"This is how character is built," said Ruben,

But Diogen wanted none of it. All he wanted, he said, was to be his own person.

"Whether you like it or not, brother, is none of my concern."

Diogen also said, "The President wasn't so kind to his enemies, from what I've heard."

To which Mona answered, to Ruben's delight, "The President hated violence, but he understood that in the case of fascism, force can only be fought with force. I imagine it's quite hard to just ignore a Nazi and pretend he doesn't exist."

"There are no more Nazis, it's over, why can't we just move on into the future?" said Diogen. "Better than all this constant revisiting of the past!"

"No more Nazis?" Ruben said. "That's what you think."

Chapter 5

ONE WOULD THINK that the inhabitants of the village in which Ruben and Diogen were born would have to love chewing rock if they were to survive. For there was only the sky, blue and bare of clouds all year round, the cutting winter wind, and the violence of the summer sun. And rock. Everywhere. If it's true what they say and one carries the landscapes of their ancestors in their bodies, then Ruben and Diogen were made of stark stone that, although beaten by the winds, lifts its face to the sun.

The eldest of five children, a pair of twins included, Ruben was the only who had gone to school. He had learned to read and write, and completed the studies that were available in the village, but when the time came for secondary school, it was too far for him to go. The nearest one was fifteen kilometers on foot, or on a mule, if you had one, and they did not. So Ruben remained in his village, helping the family earn a livelihood by growing tobacco. Then his mother had another baby, and the baby got sick. There was a cough at first, a faint cough rising from its tiny lungs, and then the cough worsened until it sounded like the howling winds outside. It was winter and the snow had gripped the ground. The doctor, who usually made his rounds once every two weeks when the weather was good, had not been around for over a month; they heard that the doctor's mule had broken a leg, and patients had to go to him to get looked at. The doctor was in the same town as the secondary school, and there was a mountain between here and there. So Ruben's parents decided to send their eldest son with their youngest one, to find the doctor.

"He will know what to do," they said of their son. "He has some learning."

Ruben walked half the way, feeling the baby breathe under his coat. They had tied it to him with a shawl, and he kept its head covered with the collar of his jacket. An aunt was supposed to meet him in the town, put them up, and give milk for the baby. The wind went right through Ruben, and he was sure the boy would die. Ruben himself fell into a fever and was in a nightmarish reverie for five nights and six days, his feet crunching snow, the baby's rasp on his chest; walking with great effort, but remaining in the same spot on a windy peak next to a church whose crucifix burned his eyes against the blinding sky. But the baby survived and regained full health. Some say that it was the natural order of things—for while Ruben and the baby were gone, their home had caught fire and the family perished in the flames. The rest of the family's sacrifice had meant that the baby's life was spared and its energy restored.

As soon as Ruben recovered, he left the baby boy in town and walked back to the village to bury the cinders and the scorched corpses into the stony ground. Ruben stood at the door of their house, watching as the wind moved the ashy remnants of the household from one spot to another; a whirlwind of soot danced around and Ruben wondered which part of their once-lives was contained in those breaths of air. He once told Rosa about it, retold the story in scattered detail. That he'd found the snake skins the twins had collected over the years and displayed on the windowsill like luminous ghosts, found them on the grass some two hundred meters from the house; that the neighbors said the fireplace must have been left open, allowing a spark to fall on a rug that must have caught alight; that there was a wild wind that blew the fire into a howling dragon that swallowed the sleeping family; that they'd heard his mother scream. That he'd found their faces unrecognizable in his mind, that somehow for him, his family members, although dead, had simply disappeared, as if in a dream. He walked once again, back to town, leaving the house behind him like a wound, seared and haunted. He never went back. Two years later World War II broke out and Ruben went to fight for the Partisans.

After returning from the war, Ruben saw Diogen through school and completed various apprenticeships as a machinist and started working in a factory. He tried to instill the spirit of the revolution in Diogen, the faith in the cause of progress and sovereignty and liberty, but even in his youngest days, Diogen never showed interest. When Ruben was twenty-five, he met Rosa, who rented a room in a stone house in one of the old neighborhoods where the steep streets were laid with shiny cobblestones. There was a fig tree in the garden that gave thick oozing fruit in August. Ruben and Rosa met and realized they had served in different units, but had both taken part in a monumental end-of-war battle, up in the forests of Šar Mountain, where the front line with the German soldiers had been.

Chapter 6

ROSA ARRIVED AT the shop at 6:00am every day, undid the padlock and pushed up the metal blinds; then she made coffee and sat quietly until the delivery men came. She spent thirty minutes putting everything in order. The shelves were organized first by the category of product, then within that category, color—from dark to light, left to right—and size—small to large, left to right. An undulating rainbow electrocardiogram of shelf life. When she was satisfied with the order, Rosa watered the two-dozen spider plants that cascaded down a metal plant holder, a torrent of striped green. She sang to them as she poured and they drank. Rosa only ever had spider plants, and was repeatedly questioned on why she only had one type of plant, always by the same people, who'd either inadvertently forget the answer or did not know what else to talk about. Rosa was not prone to chitchat, though she engaged in it if prompted, for the sake of friendliness. But she always answered in the same way: "Spider plants reduce indoor air pollution. And this way, I know how to look after one thing well."

Rosa was meticulous in everything she did. She dusted, displayed, handled, wrapped, and handed over the objects with equal attention, the attention of a sculptor shaping a piece of marble; she was neat in the way she put things into plastic bags, never made a mistake when pushing the big gray buttons of the enormous till, or when giving change. Some would just stand in a corner and watch Rosa do whatever she was doing, for she was so engrossed in any given activity that she exuded calm to anyone who was in her presence. The shop was a place people went when they needed a sense of certainty, order, clarity, as well as the latest collected works of the President.

Rosa was also one of the honored female Partisans, for she had been an extraordinary soldier. An anecdote was often repeated in the post-war years that illustrated Rosa's ingenuity and sense of clarity in even the most dangerous, exasperating situations. Having fought with few resources on a snowy plateau against the relentless and well-armed Germans, the Partisans decided to retreat. It was January, there was snow up to their knees, and they had to cross a river to reach safety. Some of the first in line stepped into the water fully clothed in their uniforms of thick wool; the river was neck-deep. Rosa shouted for them to stop. Some carried on, as if in a dream, others stopped and said, "What is it, Comrade Rosa?"

Rosa said, "We should all undress and put our clothes on top of our heads and cross the river naked. We need to keep our clothes dry, otherwise we won't survive in soaked clothes in this temperature."

And this is what they did. Those soldiers who had gone in clothed did not last long. Their feet bled, leaving crimson prints in the snow, until they could walk no more. Their comrades carried them as far as they could, but they could not survive.

Growing up, Rosa was, she was always told, the shame of the family. Her mother, Lucia, had tried all she could to provoke a miscarriage when she found out she was pregnant. The family lived in a village, and Rosa was the eighth child. Lucia was already forty-two. The village thought this to be an indecent age for pregnancy. Women were not supposed to be copulating at that age, not even for procreation. So Lucia threw herself off any height she deemed to be promising of injury; onto haystacks from balconies, down hills into valleys, off the bed in the morning, causing a loud thump to awaken all the children sleeping on the floor. But Rosa clung on, buried inside the saffron uterus, immersed in the amniotic fluid that tasted of velvet and caramel. Each bump to her was felt as a jolting need to regain the watery equilibrium, and it was here that Rosa first understood what it takes to survive: endless adaptation and keeping a steady center. (When the time came for delivery, Rosa took a straight line toward the light and emerged with little fuss.)

Lucia wore large dresses and avoided company. Except she couldn't avoid Bisera, the Roma woman. Bisera, whose name meant "pearl," like her string of incorruptibly white teeth that drew people to her immediately, arrived in the village twice a year with bands of Roma who came to harvest the everlasting flowers, also known as immortelle. The Roma made a golden oil from it or sold it in dry, fragrant bunches. Others came to pick tobacco. When Bisera came, the two women sat under the mulberry tree. Lucia would spread a tablecloth on a wooden stump and bring out the copper coffee pot and cups and Turkish delights and rose water juice. And since Bisera came every year, she had followed all of Lucia's pregnancies, save one that took place during a war. When Lucia was pregnant with Uncle Viktor, Bisera said, "You have a man-woman inside, look after him well." When she was pregnant with Rosa, but hiding it, Bisera said, "This one will be the strongest of all, no matter how hard you try to deny her, she will survive everything." Lucia looked at her and cried a tiny bit, aware that the neighbors might be watching.

When Rosa was born, the older children took turns to put their hands on her mouth to stifle her cries. The neighbors would come by and say, "We heard a baby wail in your house," and Aunt Mara, aged eight at the time, would respond, "No, there's no baby here, you are mistaken." Rosa would tell this story on each of her birthdays, chuckling. Lucia was perennially angry. She gave the children beatings for the slightest mischief. Rosa spent days up a mulberry tree, sitting in the branches until nightfall, in flight from her mother's ire. When Rosa went on her first date, aged fifteen, Lucia chased her with a stick to beat the indecency out of her. Because the most indecent thing that could possibly happen in a village had happened to her: her eldest daughter, Božena, her name something akin to the divine, or a goddess, had two illegitimate children in two years, from two different men. One of whom was married. It was a sin.

Lucia went to church and prayed to the crucified Jesus and the silent Virgin, and thought, At least the Virgin cried and suffered because her son was a prophet and wanted to save humanity, look at me, oh dear Lord Jesus, save me from sin, sin that is not even mine. Thus she whispered into her rosary, Hail Mary, Mother of God, while Jesus hung suspended above her, plastic blood all over him, exhausted.

"Sin can be viewed as any thought or action that endangers the ideal relationship between an individual and God. Or as any diversion from the perceived ideal order for human living. To sin has been defined as 'to miss the mark'," the priest had said. And the village said that Božena's children, born out of wedlock, were sin. She had missed the mark. So Lucia decided to regulate decency the only way she knew—beating sin out of her children with a stick.

Rosa and the other children often found refuge at Aunt Rosa's, her namesake who cooked up herbs for medicine and stored them in used eggshells. The villagers went to her with various ailments, and Rosa went to her for her soft nature and wild kitchen. Aunt Rosa had no husband or children, but the village accepted this, since she dedicated herself to alchemy.

Mona remembered Aunt Rosa as a body in a bed in a small room in her grandmother's house, waiting to die. Rosa always made her go in and say hello, but Mona feared the stale smell and the looming walls of her room. "Aunt Rosa was a force of life when she was young," Rosa said. "She was impetuous and impatient, but also insightful and immediate. She lost her eyesight at fifty. A piece of propelled eggshell had buried itself in her eyeball and eventually, both eyes were infected. Thereafter, Aunt Rosa could only see shadows." But Aunt Rosa carried on riding her bicycle, feeling the way with a long stick, and went berry and mushroom picking. It was Lucia's job to go through Aunt Rosa's harvest upon her return from the forest, to separate nourishment from death.

Rosa's memories, which she shared with Mona at bedtime, took place before and during World War II. After that the President had unified the Nation, and everyone went on to help build it from the ashes of destruction.

Chapter 7

MONA IS SPRAWLED across the park sofa. She can see the wisp of a cloud threaded into the blue of the sky. She can see the tree branches moving. The silver birch leaves shimmer like coins. The vast cedar holds out its many black arms for birds to rest on. The cypress points downward; the neighborhood children used its low shadowy branches to sit on when they played "house." They had many plastic toys, but what they loved best were the leftover ice lolly sticks, which they called "little people." Mona used to play it too. They drew two dot eyes and various expressions to make different characters, dressed them in sweets wrappers, and were diligent about collecting wrappers for outfits. They made lunch for the little people out of crushed leaves and grass, mashing the ingredients with stones and pond water and soil.

The park had once been the wondrous forest of Mona's life. She spent hours, all her free time, hiding in bushes and sitting on tree branches. The cypress was still one of her favorites, for its branches didn't resist her, offered themselves to her. The children had collected discarded bits of furniture from various local dumps, and arranged it in the bushy, concealed part of the park, creating a living room of sorts. There was an old sofa, an armchair with residues of pink flowers on the parts that had not been worn out by sitting bodies, and a small coffee table with a picture of a man watching the seashore. They sat around playing house and their roles shifted from parents to children to animals and back. That was when Mona was little. She would go out in the early afternoons, when everyone was having their prescribed rest time and children were not allowed to play outside, from three to five. It was called "house order" in the meaning of being "orderly," and not "to be ordered," though in reality the residents were ordered not to go outside. If children did go outside and made noise between the designated hours, disgruntled neighbors emerged on balconies or descended the stairs in slippers, hair messy and mouths billowing with rage. They yelled at them to go home, or threatened to call their parents. So Mona would sneak out and go down to the park when no one was outside, and she would sit in silence or play voicelessly, mouthing the dialogue between the little people. Daddy sometimes shouted; Mommy shouted back. The children sat in a corner, quiet. Or she would lie down on the sofa and watch the canopy of trees above her.

They say that trees are alive; not just in the way that can be observed, with the leaves growing and falling off. But that they are alive with families and communities, and that they are intelligent. And if they are damaged, or their leaves start to get chewed on by say, a caterpillar, or a grazing giraffe, some trees give off a toxic scent that repels the animal eating it and warns the other trees to release the same scent and defend themselves. Mona read this in a book. Trees, it said, work together. When they are friends, their branches grow as far as they can to touch each other, as if with fingertips. There was such a union, a love union, really, between a linden and an oleander tree on a street in her mother's village. The linden grew in a garden on the left side of the street, the oleander on the right, and their branches stretched above the garden walls and bent toward each other, their leaves touching mid-air, mid-street, making an arch of pink and yellow flowers, and they perfumed the air with gentle affection. They held hands, but never went any further toward each other, for they knew that the light and the air on the opposite side was already needed, and taken. And that is what the President instructs us to do, thought Mona. To work together. To build our community, to honor our families, and to protect the unity of our country. Mona had felt this, the drive, the need, the meaning of the revolutionary project of the Nation alive in her breast. But lately, she had other things on her mind, and they flooded everything, and she could do little to fight it.

Ruben often sat Mona down to tell her the story of the Nation. He had told her this story many times—he had told her that the streets of her hometown were mostly made of gray stone, and there was an ochre mud mixture that was used for some of the facades. Ruben had told her, at bedtime when she was small, and at lunch when she grew, that the first road leading into town was paved when the President announced his first visit. Before that, the roads were dusty bare ground, trodden by mules and wooden clogs. Upon hearing of the visit, Ruben said, the town council decided that ten young local men should go to the hill above town, the hill facing the direction of the newly paved road, and spell out in white chalk rocks—dug out from the earth around the city, the rugged earth that brimmed with nothing but stone—We Love You, President. One of the youth chosen for the task was Ruben.

They were heavy rocks, Ruben said, and the youth sweated and strained as they worked. They had to ensure that the words were all leveled equally, that the "We" wasn't bigger than "You." It took a whole week. The sun was a mallet on their foreheads, the skin on their necks turning into copper leather. There was a small delay when they discovered a spelling mistake; instead of Love they had written "Luve." Luckily, the town administrator, who looked up from the town center every afternoon to see how the work was going, noticed, and the mistake was quickly corrected. When their work was done, the young men got a round of handshakes, pats on the back, and a barbecued lunch with beer as their reward. Ruben was always proud of himself for being part of the project, and Mona was proud of Ruben.

The sign stood there like a focused thought, Mona thought, and every time anyone gazed round the city that thought would vibrate in their mind. The President was like a divine watcher, the bearer of ultimate values, and that which remained pure when all else became soiled, said Ruben. When Mirza bullies Toni at school, the President loves me, Mona thought. When Ana rejects Edin, the President still loves me. When Ruben and Diogen fight over Diogen's life choices and his needing to "pull his socks up," the President still loves us, Mona thought.

At school, Mona learned stories about the President's childhood, about his modest home in a village in the mountains and saw photographs of him cutting keys with a smile, galaxies of sparks flying off the iron wheel. The President repeatedly spoke of the need to look after the country, and each other, to obey parents and teachers, and to keep the country's unity as the utmost priority. Brotherhood and Unity, Brotherhood and Unity, Brotherhood and Unity. School children sang songs that promised to never stray off his path, songs that promised that he could count on everyone to fight for peace, should the need arise. One of the songs that Mona was fond of, went:

Some doubt our conviction and think that we are
going in the wrong direction,
because we listen to vinyl records and play rock,
But somewhere in us sits battle's flame
and I tell you what I know well:
You can count on us.

Each classroom and each official space in the country had a picture of the President on the wall. On her first day of school, as pairs of students sat in rows of desks, the teacher came in to class and announced: "Children. Some of you may have heard of God, and that he exists. Well, he doesn't." He then went to distributed chocolate bars, one per child. No more was said. That same day, Mona read a story in her school book about two boys who fought over who the President was gazing at from one of those pictures. Each was insisting "me, me," until the teacher came up and said, "Don't fight. The President is watching over us all."

In his photographed presence, school children were not to wear hats, nothing that would cover their heads. They were not allowed to chew gum, because that was both rude and stank of rotten capitalism, something that lived outside of their borders and bore a fiendish mix of fascination, fantasy, and loathing, according to their teacher. They were taught that the struggle of their forebearers was what brought them to where they were, and they had to honor that struggle, always. The struggle that had built the Nation. The struggle that meant ethnic, national and religious differences had been overcome in the name of building the Nation. God could be worshipped, if one insisted on it, but it was not acceptable to feel that one's God was better than someone else's. Brotherhood and Unity, above all. The Nation was forged out of the antifascist struggle, the struggle for equality. The only country to have defended itself by its own forces, Ruben said. The only European country to have had no foreign army on its soil at the end of World War II, teachers said. Mona knew of these struggles. Understood that she was part of them, that she came from the bodies of those who had been on the edge of death in order to provide that freedom to all. When she went to see her very old grandmother as a small child, Mona observed the crucified Christ on her wall, with the picture of the President right next to it. Christ bled too, there was never a smiling Christ, but the President was sometimes smiling. Mona had even seen a picture of the President sunbathing, looking very relaxed.

The Nation watched films about brave warriors who traipsed snowy mountains for liberty and got so frostbitten that they had to cut off each others' toes, with nothing but homemade brandy to anesthetize them. The Nation bit their lips as the movie soldiers applied army knives to each others' purple toes, and each time they prayed to a God they knew didn't exist that the movie should end differently. They professed love from the hilltop. And they held struggle in their hearts.

Chapter 8

ONE OF THE WAYS the Nation expressed gratitude for its freedom, and furthered the allegiance to the foundations of the country, was by having each generation of children take the Pioneer Oath. Thus, everyone was wedded to the country, its soil, its heart. The Pioneer Oath was taken at the Partisan Necropolis. Ruben remembered Mona taking her oath here. A sea of red neckerchiefs knotted at the gullet. Small blue envelope caps each bearing a red five-point glass star. The envelope cap like an origami piece, needing to be puffed out before being affixed to a child's head. Ruben thought of the factories where they produced the caps and the neckerchiefs, rivers of blue and red bleeding from the stabbing needles of the sewing machines.

Parents and siblings watched with pride. If a family had a camera—and most did not—they took photos for themselves, and for those who did not. Children stood lined up in long rows, silent and almost breathless; words boomed from the loudspeakers:

Today, when I become a pioneer,
I give my pioneer's word of honor:
That I will work and study diligently,
that I will respect my parents and elders,
and be a loyal and honest friend,
who keeps his word.
That I will love our country,
cherish the brotherhood and unity
of all her peoples,
and appreciate all the people of the world
who want freedom and peace.

Each child was given a red carnation. Ruben watched Mona inhaling its powdery clove smell. A carnation is a common flower, Ruben thought, but it is a beautiful one. Its soft head feels like silk against your lips, its smell unobtrusive and warm. A carnation was thought to be the flower of incarnation, and coronation. In the case of the new Pioneers both were true, Ruben felt, they were becoming something else on this day, crowned in glory, incarnated into the next generation of the country's guardians.

The Partisan Necropolis was also the place where Ruben took Rosa on their first date. They walked toward the enormous monument etched into the pine-covered hill in the southern part of town. Ruben took Rosa's hand as they strolled through the collection of terraces that spilled down the slope, just stone and water and green. There were twisting pathways, fountains that became waterways, all ending in a large, still pool in the shape of a tear, right at the bottom. There was frogspawn in the tear; in springtime children submerged their hands to feel for the slimy texture. Flowers and celestial formations were carved in the stone around them.

Ruben and Rosa were passionate about the monument. It was built by a famed architect and celebrated everything that the country stood for: the Partisan struggle, the deaths of many for the freedom of many, the new life that came from that sacrifice. Ruben and Rosa, who had both forged much of their souls in the war, felt that the monument spoke to them personally. And Ruben told Rosa the story of the monument, which he had been told by the architect himself. Ruben had internalized Bogdan Bogdanovic's words, and he narrated them in the way he had once heard the architect deliver them. He waved his hands as he told the story, a glimmer in his eye: "The stone was worked by stonemasons from an island that was nothing but stone. There, the stonemasons' tradition was centuries' old, and required great skill and strength and discipline, both of the body and the mind. But what it required most of all was working in unison with others. The masons came in a group, led by a so-called Uncle, a kind of maestro, a great conductor. He was the man who would report to the parents and fiancées what the men did and how well they worked. This was very important. The honor and the image of the island and the community and the family depended on the decent behavior of the stonemasons."

Ruben wagged his finger at this point, just like Bogdan had when he told the same story to a young Ruben. "The spot from which the Uncle led the work was in front of the group, and the men lined up in order to face him. The summer heat meant that they could only work from dawn to just after breakfast, and from sunset to midnight. The architect was anxious about whether what he had envisaged would work, would at all be possible. He went to the ancient bridge that was the pride and joy of the town. It was several hundred years old, and made of stone, and he touched it as if trying to get answers to his own questions from the old bridge maker. And so, in his fingertips, through his skin, the architect carried the wisdom from one stone to the other. Sharing the memory stored in the mineral. And how sad that we use stone to name all the things that don't have feelings, that don't have a soul. If you touch and caress a pebble, a piece of rock, a boulder, its textures will tell you things that the world cannot hear. And this is what the stonemasons knew."

Ruben got close to Rosa, as if revealing a secret, and whispered, "They understood stone, and its character, and they could hear the voice of all the different types of stone. And Bogdan Bogdanović heard it too. This is how he described it—he said that every piece of stone reverberated like a musical instrument. He knew, of course, that different types make different sounds, and the softer the stone, the deeper its tone. It's paradoxical, and slightly comical, that the hardest granite had a piercing pitch, marble sings with a slight mezzo soprano, and limestone, the most musical of stones, has a beautiful, velvety alto. Practiced stonemasons can hear even more. 'Each one sings its own song,' said one of them, convinced that each piece was a being in its own right."

Ruben breathed out, enchanted by the invisible work going on around him.

"The work of the stonemasons was akin to some alchemy, an invocation of the spirits. The architect told of how he saw acetylene lamps, or carbon lamps from the past century, a dim light and even dimmer shadows. And in the light, something mysterious was happening. The gray Uncle, his hair static and pointing to all four sides of the world, is spellbinding, like a wizard, like a genie who had emerged from the stone. Out of the blue, he lifts the hammer and chisel. The masons lift their hammers in a holy hush. A silence comes up that reveals all the sounds of the night: crickets, nightingales, the murmur of the river in the distance. One of the masons starts up the wordless melody, nasal and mystical, a ritual of stone worshippers. The Uncle's hammer strikes the rhythm. He hits the piece that is in front of him, and immediately they are chiseling together in harmony. When the melody starts to rise, everyone is singing, the sound of the chisel becomes deafening. When it lowers, the sounds become softer. This is how the pieces manage to have the same form engraved into them, how the lines have consistency between each piece." Ruben pointed around them, at the walls. "When the chiseling started, the rhythm developed on every stone instrument, and, every arm movement, every posture, so that the entire orchestra functioned as its own metronome. And when the pounding started to scatter—a sign that concentration was dropping—the Uncle lifted his hammer sternly. This meant that the work had to pause for a minute, and that the beat must be synchronized all over again. They then waited for the warble of the man who produces the melody, and the Uncle's first strike.

"This monument was built with love," Ruben said to Rosa on that first date. "And devotion. And knowledge, not just of the work and the skill of hitting stone, but the knowledge of things beyond the eye. The masons sang a wordless song, one that maybe went back to a time that preceded language."

The architect believed, along with many alchemist-builders, that limestone was the child of the Sun and the Moon, and that it was meant for making celestial forms. The Necropolis held flowers, suns, moons, planets, stars. The monument sang toward the town, and to the heavens, and the town sang back at it. And it was where Ruben went to honor his important moments, among these unseen worlds, among the mineral constellations.

Chapter 9

ROADS, RAILWAYS, FACTORIES, and every other part of the Nation's infrastructure were built by tens of thousands of young volunteers, euphoric in their willingness to participate in what was known as Youth Work Actions, or YWA. The President had called upon the young, and the young answered with love and labor. In 1946, the first railway, 88 kilometers long, was built in 190 days, thanks to 62,268 members of the Nation. Foreign youths also took part, joining the local brigades: two dozen of them were French, Spanish, Danish; there was a sprinkling of Austrians, Belgians, and Indians; a dot of the Dutch and two Mexican women; Polish, Czechoslovak, Greek, Hungarian, Rumanian, Bulgarian, and Albanian brigades also participated. And, like a bee works with its fellows to build up a hive, under the watchful eye of the queen, the youth of the country passed buckets from hand to hand, struck the earth with spades in unison, pushed wheelbarrows, singing the songs of liberation and the national struggle all the while, the songs and their regular rhythms giving wind to the sails of productive labor and the birth of their new country. In return for their work, they received licenses (after learning to drive during their free time), and training in radio and theater, literacy courses were run, as well as stitching and domestic work seminars. Thus numerous roads and key railway connections were built, with volunteers laying kilometers upon kilometers of asphalt and tracks. The National Film Studios, numerous factories, and entire towns were built during the first twenty years of the Nation, thanks to these volunteers. When anyone recalled any part of the YWA, it was done so with dreamy nostalgia, a feeling for the good old times, their sense of purpose and union keen and passionate. The numbers swelled to hundreds of thousands, young men and women alike; the great writer Miroslav Krleža described their effort as that of "children with torches in their hands, who had ... brought light into our darkness with a true torch of the ages, handing it over to the future generations."

Not so for Diogen. He hated every minute of it—the enthusiasm, the physical labor, the getting dirty. He had gone thinking it would be a good idea, a way to get away from life. He found the socializing tiresome, the dancing tedious, and the only thing that had kept him going was the repetitive pounding of spade against soil—thump! breathe, thump! breathe, thump!—when he did forestation work; that's when his mind was calm. He enjoyed burying the fragile roots of the new trees into the warm soil, handling them gently, talking to them, telling them to grow tall and not be shy. But at night, as he lay down, his eyes stinging and his limbs feeling as if they were made of cast iron, thoughts would come swarming back, his mind a restless beehive and his head would spin like the inside of a cement mixer.

In fact, after Diogen's return from the Youth Work Action, Ruben would throw a special welcome back party for his brother in the shop. Ruben saw the YWA as a coming of age moment in Diogen's life, the event that would finally make him a man. Or if not make him one, show him the way to become one! He remembered his own YWA experiences, in the post war years, when hundreds of young men and women went to rebuild the devastated country; the youth had been inspired by the wartime efforts of the first Youth Brigades, which had helped the Partisan soldiers by harvesting fruits and vegetables and grains and transporting crops to hospital units tending the wounded. Ruben remembered his first love, which he had experienced then. Young Mersiha was from the southern region of the new country. Oh how they glanced at each other across the campfire that was built every evening, the orange light of the flames caressing Mersiha's soft cheeks. They would move around the fire in the traditional circle dance, and sometimes he and Mersiha would step out at the same time, their feet tired from the day's work and the dancing, but their spirits fresh and energized. They'd sit on the ground and watch the dancers' legs hopping and Ruben entertained thoughts of holding Mersiha's hand, giving way to his desire, but he could not muster the courage to do it. It just was not right, it would have harmed the girl's honor and reputation, both of which were of utmost importance. It was no good for girls to go around holding hands or kissing, oh no, Ruben thought, not like today when any young lady can get up to no good and no one even cares. "We build the railway—the railway builds us," went the motto. Ruben reminisced, a sigh escaping from his chest as he thought about Diogen's return.

Ruben still woke in the night sometimes, when it snowed and the wind howled, having dreamed of his brother's tiny mouth gasping for life. In a way, Ruben never understood how Diogen had survived, and how Diogen's illness was what had saved the two boys from the fire. There were many things that Ruben placed outside his comprehension—he could not discern what had been a blessing and what had been a curse. All he knew for certain was that their lives were what they were now—orderly, respectable, calm—thanks to the President's benevolence. And for that he was grateful every day. But Ruben saw Diogen as too soft, too moody, too undisciplined, too reclusive. It was time for Diogen to take part in society. In less than a month his military service would begin, and it was no good if Diogen went into the army as soft as he was. It was, Ruben thought, time to help build him, even if Diogen did not seem interested in being built. As a boy, after Ruben returned from the war, he noted that Diogen had developed some traits that Ruben did not like, such as singing long warbling songs until he was red in the face, but he had allowed it for he had read that passionate crying and singing by children was good for their lung development.

"But," Ruben said to himself, "the time has come for Diogen to give up these boyish tendencies."

Chapter 10

THE ENTIRE FAMILY lived upstairs from the shop, in a three-bedroom apartment. It had been Ruben, Rosa, Diogen, and Mona, but upon Diogen's departure for the YWA, Ruben and Diogen's great uncle, Robinson, moved in with the family. Robinson was eighty-nine and partially blind with wild white hair growing out of his ears. He had always lived alone. Ruben had long felt a duty to go and check on him, and Rosa made food for him occasionally. But when Robinson started to fall over with increasing frequency, which ultimately resulted in a broken hip, they decided that the time had come for them to take him in.

Robinson—originally known as Ilija—became known as Robinson after spending years living in the wild on a barren little island where nothing had managed to survive, except for him. He built his own raft, then a little boat, and went into the woods at night to catch rabbits for food, or fished under a lamp, as fishermen do, and he lived inside a cane hut that he built. This is how he told it, though no one really understood how he'd managed to survive on an island made entirely of rock and nothing else. Robinson left many gaps in the patchwork tale of his life. But one day, and no one knows why, he decided to return. The family had thought he was dead, so there was some fainting when this disheveled, deeply suntanned man returned and announced himself. Robinson had also fought with the Partisans in the war, but, he said, "Disgusted by war and humanity, I decided to stay in solitude and isolation!" After telling people where he had been, the neighbors started to say, "Oh here comes Robinson Crusoe," or if he walked into a bar they'd say, "Hello Robinson, how's it going today," and so the nickname stuck, and Robinson liked it.

He now occupied Diogen's bedroom, since Diogen had been away and would be going to the army soon. The idea was that the two men would share until Diogen's departure. Ruben was slightly nervous about what Diogen might think of this arrangement when he returned, and Rosa was convinced that it was a terrible idea. For Robinson had not only brought himself and his broken hip to their home, he had also brought The Invention: a self-powered engine that Robinson claimed was the most advanced machine ever invented. He, however, refused to reveal its purpose.

Robinson woke up every day at 4:00am, started on his exercise routine, lifting two water filled bottles like weights, and then washed himself with salt water, which he made by pouring lots of kitchen salt into a bucket. He then put on his woolen hat. He was afraid of the draught on his wet hair—the popular belief was that inflammation of the brain was a looming possibility if a draught caught one's wet hair (and Robinson claimed to have spent the years on the island in that very same woolen hat, much to Ruben's visible disgust). He breakfasted on nuts and fruit and a large chunk of pork fat, and set about oiling The Invention. This was at around 4:45, and as the sun came up behind the mountain peaks, Robinson's room and the entire flat were permeated with the smell of industrial oil, and the sound of Robinson's hushed chattering, a sort of pillow talk to The Invention.

The windows had to be kept open all day and all night. During the day, The Invention was covered up with a plastic sheet. Mona thought she could hear it purr ever so lightly.

Ruben kept saying, "I don't know how long we can keep this up."

"Well, he's here now," Rosa would respond. "We can't very well throw him out."

One day Ruben said, "I tried to get him to move The Invention to the balcony, so that it doesn't stink so much inside, but he says it's top secret and it can't be outside. He keeps the door to his room closed all day so that no one can get a glimpse of the stupid thing! He'll get toxic fume poisoning, sleeping with it so close. We'll all get toxic fume poisoning!"

Chapter 11

"PSST."

Mona was studying in the living room. Robinson had left the door of his room ajar and when Mona looked at him, he beckoned with his forefinger. She got up and walked to his room. Apart from the overwhelming smell of industrial oil, the room stank of Robinson's cigarettes, which he rolled by hand with five different filters inserted into the rolling paper, all of which he made himself, out of rice and cotton wool and cardboard, claiming that this was a sure way to ward off lung cancer, citing his advanced age and full smoking habit as evidence that this was so.

"What is it?" Mona asked, feeling a little nauseous from the mixture of bad odors and thinking that the hair in Robison's ears had grown bushier overnight.

He stood in the middle of the room with a ten-inch cigarette hanging from the corner of his mouth, like a strange smoking beak. He wore a dark blue boiler suit and his thick glasses enlarged his cataract-infused eyes so that they looked like framed lakes.

"Did you know, Mona, that I am a Stoic?"

Mona said nothing.

"Do you know what a Stoic is?"

Mona said yes.

"You should learn from me. I am a man of experience," said Robinson.

Mona looked around at the state of the room. He had thrown the mattress off the bed, was sleeping on the wooden slats. For the last few days he'd only been eating bread and drinking water, something he claimed he did every month for a few days.

"You see all this, sleeping like this, taking nothing but bread and water—I am preparing for when the great wheel of Fortune decides to hand out its spiky deal!" He moved around the room. "The spiky deal always comes! You'd think, here I am in comfort, I have a bed, your mother cooks me stuffed peppers and all kinds of delicious meals, and I should just lie down and enjoy myself, right?"

Mona shrugged.

"No! What if tomorrow I have to live in a shelter and eat nothing but bread all day long? How do you think I'd take to that, eh, accustomed as I am to a life of comfort?"

"I don't know," Mona said.

"Not too well. I would be used to good things only. I'd sit with my head in my hands and regard a piece of bread as a dry, useless thing. But this way, I practice, like a soldier in peacetime. For one never knows when misfortune will strike, and strike it always will!"

Mona was silent.

"But that's not what I have called you in here for, dear girl," said Robinson. "You are here because the moment has come. The moment has come."

"What moment?"

"This, my girl," he said, pointing to the machine, "this will change the world!"

Robinson yanked the sheet off The Invention, like a magician unveiling his trick, and Mona would not have been surprised if a bunch of bunnies had been revealed, or one of those people suddenly finding their body parts in several boxes. But instead there stood a thing with many cogs and wheels, lashed together metal sheets, and a large telescope at the one end of it and a projection lens on the other. The Invention looked like a sort of mechanical aardvark, Mona thought. She circled around it and it seemed to breathe through its many-colored wires.

"Oh wow. What's it for? Will you finally tell me?" asked Mona.

The machine dripped with oil and its parts winked at her with the scarce flickering light. She had been bemused by and curious about The Invention, unlike Ruben and Rosa, who cursed it under their breath. But Mona was the first to see it. Outside, the sky swelled with granite-colored clouds. A bolt of lightning was followed by a deep metallic clang of thunder. Dogs fell into a line of barking, one after another. Fleshy drops of rain knocked like knuckles on the tin windowsill.

"Ah, my dear, that's just it," Robinson said as he closed the window. "No one could have known about it before I copyrighted my baby. But I did, I have managed to do it. I finally got the letter with the confirmation. No one can steal the idea from me now, that was the danger you see, not that they could have done anything with the idea anyway since this machine is much too clever for any idiot in this town to understand. But look at what happened to Nikola Tesla, our great scientist—such a clever man, but destroyed by the greed and stupidity of capitalists, and ultimately his own lack of brains when it came to business. Man is a dangerous animal." He lifted his finger and a long strand of ash fell off his cigarette onto the floor. "What it does—and you will be the first person to know about it because you are young and the young are smart—is that it helps you look into the future."

Mona stopped circling. "No way."

"Oh yes way, dear girl. But you must tell no one yet. They'll think I'm mad," he whispered, tapping his head with his forefinger. "And then it's all over, they can remove my copyright and steal The Invention."

"It can really see into the future? I thought that there was no set future to see, that we built the future with cooperation and our hard work?"

"Nonsense," said Robinson. "The future is written out in the stars. You can do whatever you like, but what's been set down ahead for you, no one can change. I saw that when I was living on the island, all alone, eating weeds and whatever I could catch. Our destinies are all mapped out for us, like the galaxies are set in the sky."

Mona gulped. "Why did you live alone on the island?"

"Ah, it was a whim of youth, I was disillusioned, I had started working for a great engineering company and I had this wonderful idea, for a space project, and they told me I was in cuckoo land, and I told them all to go to hell and went on a boat and found the island and lived there. Those were the best years of my life. It's where I had the idea for The Invention. But I had to come back to civilization, if that's what you can call it, to find the means to build this magical machine. And here it is."

He drew the blinds down so that there was just a tiny bit of gloomy light lingering in the room. Thunder rolled outside, like a sheet of metal being shaken. Mona stood and watched as Robinson attached a head torch to his forehead and fumbled in a little box until he pulled out a tiny key. He missed the keyhole at the back of The Invention several times due to his weak vision, but when he finally inserted the key, the machine came to life with a storm of whirling and clicking and hissing noises and a huge spotlight lit the back wall of the room.

"Oh wow!" said Mona.

Robinson smiled. More thunder sounded outside, the dogs stopped barking, and all the lights went out.

Chapter 12

THE DAY BEFORE his welcome back party, a dirty, sweaty, and sullen Diogen arrived at the town station with his knapsack. He wanted to shower and sleep and then go out to his secret spot on the riverbank, to sit under the honeyberry tree, eat its tiny purple fruit, and sing. Diogen loved to sing, and he loved to sing opera, and what he'd loved most about the YWA was that he could escape for an hour every day into the empty fields and sing at the top of his lungs. No one knew if he sung well, or if he sung badly, and neither did Diogen, but it made him feel as if he were a soaring bird, a turquoise tropical flurry of feathers in the sky. He also loved singing quiet traditional songs of love and loss, his throat trembling with a tender vibrato.

After Rosa married Ruben, Diogen discovered that singing to himself in the mirror when everyone was out of the house made him weep with joy, especially if he painted his lips red and put on a pair of Rosa's clip-on pearl earrings. Mozart's aria "Vorrei spiegarvi, oh Dio!" was possibly his favorite. He also loved to watch the teenage boys swim across the river. The boys, sometimes in groups, sometimes in pairs, swam across the foaming waves in a display of budding masculinity; the river was rough and wild, full of whirlpools, and there were rocks and caves on each side, ideal for exploring and diving. Diogen sometimes joined them, though he could only swim over to one side; he would always walk back across one of the bridges. He loved to watch the way the muscles moved in their arms, in their legs, the steadiness of their feet as they hopped between rocks, their fearlessness, the drops of water on their hair, on their eyelashes, the way they emerged unscathed from the freezing river.

The boys swam for the delight of swimming, but also to impress girls. There was one girl in particular, Sofia, a dark limbed nymph with hair the color of coal—this is how one of the boys described her—who would come down every day around noon and dive into the river elegantly. She would swim to the nearest rock and lay there sunbathing. The boys would dive around her, swim past her, shout out to each other over her, like a school of splattering fish; Sofia paid them zero attention. But there would be a moment in the day when she would throw them a glance, just before she swam back to shore and disappeared, walking off, in another boy's words, with the gait of a goddess. Diogen appreciated Sofia, liked her lack of care for the hysterical boys. But he did not care to impress her. His focus, the focus of all his songs and energy for some time now, was on Ivan Ivanovich.

Ivan lived in the old neighborhood, with his mother; his father had died in a coal mining accident some years before. Ivan was shy and softly spoken. Diogen had observed his every move, gesture, characteristic, and quality. The first time they met, on a winter night as Diogen was roaming the streets, singing under his breath, Ivan appeared in front of him, distracted by something and the two men nearly bumped into each other. Ivan said, "Oh, excuse me," and blinked, startled, and his eyes, the color of chestnuts, appeared to Diogen to be glowing more intensely than the Earth's molten core; he observed a fire inside them, and Ivan's breath, when he said excuse me, exhaling the words, enveloped Diogen and cradled him, lifting him out of the cold night. The town streets and his entire life up to that moment appeared to him mundane, dreary, perishable; everything suddenly seemed irrelevant, offensive even in its lack of significance compared to Ivan's eyes, the beauty of his being. Diogen noted the wave in his mahogany hair, the length of his slender fingers, the calluses from the hard strings of the cello—although he did not know at that time that Ivan played the cello; he saw the movement of his thigh as he stopped, the molecules of his breath as its vapor vanished into the frigid air. Diogen wished he could preserve each speck of air that surrounded Ivan and store it in a jar as an object of utter beauty.

Ivan came to the river with the boys, but made little noise. He swam across the river with ease. Diogen watched him break the waves and whirls and felt breathless with the agonizing pull of his biceps. The two men were not exactly friends, and although they spent little time interacting, they were aware of each other. Ivan knew when Diogen was there, and when he fished, if he caught several freckled trout, he would gift one to Diogen. Diogen was usually alone in his spot under the tree. He had a fishing rod, though he rarely put bait on the hook; it was really that the rod gave him the appearance of doing something, liberated him from unwanted questions of what he might be doing all alone by the river. Sometimes both Diogen and Ivan went along with the boys to explore the craggy rocks on the banks; the summer heat would lower the river, exposing the panicking crabs that scuttled away from the boys' grabbing fingers. Those were the moments Diogen cherished, for it gave him the opportunity to move in Ivan's proximity and breathe his air, and he felt as if they were performing a dance. He knew where Ivan lived, knew his daily patterns; Ivan was alive in Diogen's life through persistent, precise, involved observation.

A month had passed since Diogen had departed for the YWA, and since he had seen Ivan. The last thing he wanted was a Welcome Home, Comrade party; it was enough that his military service, a year-long prison sentence as Diogen saw it, something he could not even begin to fathom how he would survive, either physically or mentally, was due to start in three weeks. He had been putting it off for four years by doing his university degree, and mostly by Ruben's interventions through military connections, but there was no more time to bide. He now had three weeks of freedom, and he intended to spend them filling every brain cell with the image of Ivan.

He walked home through the all too familiar streets, his head down, trying to avoid greeting the tailor, the butcher, the cobbler. But a strange thing caught his eye—sheets of paper torn from a school notebook with a handwritten note reading: "The Invention—Unveiled! Come and See Your Future! Entry: 500 dinars." And their street address. Their home address: Number 23. Diogen stopped in front of one sign and re-read the note. Yes, their home address. He laughed—500 dinars was a fortune, a month's average salary. He tore off one of the notes and walked home.

Chapter 13

ROSA'S REVOLUTIONARY PATH began when she left her large family. She went into town and got a job as an assistant in a shop owned by family friends; they also boarded her in a small room. Rosa started work early. She walked a mile to reach the shop every day. It was January 1941. The winter winds could be so strong they toppled cars over in the street; under the gusts of air that felt like oceanic avalanches, Rosa could do no more than to hold on to a lamppost with both hands, her feet losing ground as the wind lifted her young body.

The shop was tiny and cold and Rosa and a colleague, another young girl from a nearby village, kept warm by building a fire in the small backyard. Over a couple of months, Rosa proved herself to be an excellent administrator and became the shop manager. The day Rosa got promoted, and as the lights in the house went out, the family friend tried to get into her bed. What the family friend did not know was that Rosa was always at the ready. She had noticed the older man gazing at her with a certain lasciviousness, that there was no lock on her door, and that he mentioned hosting several young girls before, each of whom had left inexplicably. Rosa thus decided to sleep with her pocketknife under the pillow. The folding blade was rather large when straightened, capable of halving an apple in a simple swift move. When the door creaked open that night, Rosa gripped the knife. She saw the man's silhouette and felt him touch her blanket. She jumped up straight, grabbed him by the throat, and pinned him against the wall with the knife under his Adam's apple. Her breath was hot against his and she felt her whole body radiate with fear and fury and joy. The man saw the young woman's eyes shine in the night, he didn't know if he was facing a wolf or something even wilder, but he felt the knife firm against his throat and knew that this had been a great mistake. Rosa left the next day.

The country was invaded in the spring of 1941. Local collaborators entered the streets with the invading armies and hung their flags; they rounded up people, took them away, shot other people in the streets. Rosa volunteered with a local brigade and became a brigade administrator within a month. After proving herself to be a reliable, organized, and clear-thinking individual, she was sent to serve as a messenger in the south of the country. Rosa traversed mountain paths shown to her by local shepherds. She always worked at night. If she worked in the day, she dressed as a shepherdess in case anyone caught her: a sheepskin jacket, leather slippers, wool stockings. She moved between strategic military positions, carrying tiny written notes buried inside her long black plaits, which she wrapped around her head like a wreath.

Rosa had to walk many miles inside forests and across mountains. She often said later, as did many other soldiers from that time, that the forests and the mountains were their saviors; the enemy had no knowledge of the many paths, ridges, crevasses, cliffs, and riverbeds. The locals did, and traversed them with growing expertise. They trapped and killed the enemy soldiers and took their weapons, and the resisting army thus grew, both in volunteers and weaponry, like a dark forest spirit.

It was during this time that Rosa developed her hunting skills. She learned how to catch and skin a rabbit, and how to kill a deer, and she hunted small birds. She shared her bounty with the soldiers. This was one of the rules of their struggle: to share with each other and never abandon their comrades. Rosa did not like murdering the animals, asked for God's mercy as she felt life leave their warm bodies. But she enjoyed the precision that the hunt required. She made her own traps, with pieces of wood and rubber. She knew all the edible plants, found wild rocket, wild fennel, knew where she could find nut trees and understood which berries were edible. In mushrooming months, she foraged the edible fungi. She came to know which peasants were reliable, who produced cheese and kept bees, and went to those she knew would share their food with the brigades. Rosa would load up her canvas bag and walk the shadowy forest paths with great care, her every sense attuned. She became adept at distinguishing the sounds of animals from the sounds of soldiers' boots, the way a forest animal moved, stepping lightly on the crackling twigs with four hooves and the way a human step charged and crushed the undergrowth. Once, a wild boar circled her and charged; Rosa hid in an oak tree until dawn, when the animal finally strutted away.

Rosa told this story to Mona with a great cackle, saying, "Oh, how I trembled up in that tree. The hog seemed quite aware of me, watched me with those clever eyes, and I thought, well, this is the way of the world, or at least that was the way of the world at the time. We attack, we defend, and it goes in a circle. I must have stepped on its territory. Of course it would go after me."

Mona, listening to her mother's stories, always imagined a different person, for she could not reconcile her patient, often silent mother with this young woman who had spent years in the national liberation struggle, in forests, with knives and uniforms. But, sometimes, she caught a glimpse of this person, especially when Rosa had to get rid of a wasp's nest on their balcony, or mice in the kitchen, or when she went back to her village and worked around the animals. Rosa was, then, alive in an entirely different way. She was neither cruel nor sentimental, and whenever she could be, she was kind. Inside her mother, Mona understood, was a well of action that could only manifest in the natural world, but this action sat suspended inside her domestic life. Rosa believed, Mona knew, for she had said it many times, that her duty was to be with the family and do what was necessary for the family to thrive. But it was when she was out in the elements that Rosa's spirit changed. Which is why Mona demanded that Rosa tell her stories from the war.

After three years, in 1944, Rosa had established herself as one of the key messengers in the region, and was one day summoned to see the commander of the Southern Brigade. He wore a thick woolen olive uniform with wide lapels and smoked constantly. Dark lipped and dark haired, he said, "Comrade Rosa, you are one of the best messengers of the People's Revolution. And we have an important message that must be delivered directly to Comrade Crimson." Comrade Crimson would later become the President; this was his code name at the time.

"Of course, Comrade," Rosa said. "I am honored to be chosen for such a task." She took the message and wove it into her dark hair as always, received the instructions regarding Comrade Crimson's whereabouts, put on her sheepskin gown, and set out on her journey.

The Southern Brigade's commander had informed Rosa of specific safety posts across the country. These were mostly peasant houses in the mountains. Comrade Crimson was hiding out in a cave in a town some 200 kilometers from where Rosa was. She made the first part of the journey with a local brigade, which consisted of young men and women with weathered faces and unfaltering morale. She had transport across safe areas, and walked the more dangerous parts because she could take cover more easily. She carried a handgun. Whenever she joined a brigade, it turned out they had heard of Comrade Rosa. They had heard of her dodging Italian troops in the south, and of how she escaped a bear.

One said, "What was worse, the Italians or the bear?"

Rosa smiled and said, "Both were equally difficult for me to understand."

And those listening laughed and slapped their knees and said, "Oh, Comrade Rosa, you're hard to understand, too!"

One day, Rosa killed a deer and brought it to a brigade, a group of fifty starving men and women; they claimed she had saved their lives. When she didn't kill the deer for food, the animals would watch her and she'd watch them quietly, and birds and butterflies landed on her shoulders. She slept how she always slept. After walking most of the night, she would find a suitable tree and mount a hammock of sorts between the branches, and sleep for four hours. "That's all I ever needed," she told Mona. The elevated sleeping position ensured that she was not going to be surprised in the night by soldiers, snakes, or other dangerous species. The journey to Comrade Crimson's cave lasted over three weeks. Rosa was exhausted at the end of it, for she had crossed three mountain peaks, and suffered freezing conditions on two. It was late spring, and the nights were cold and she could not light a fire for fear of attracting the enemy's attention. But this was the job Rosa knew she could not fail to complete. The whole country's destiny depended on the successful delivery of this message. That's what the commander had told her. Yet she had no idea what the message was. So, after worrying about the message getting ruined by the elements, Rosa undid her hair and took out the piece of paper and memorized the message and re-plaited it into her coal hair and wove the plaits around her head again. Seen like that, her black braids curving upon her head like a crown, her cheekbones high, her eyes nut brown and shining, her face coffee colored from the sun, the sheepskin her armor, her determination relentless, Rosa appeared like an ancient warrior, a goddess dropped from the heavens.

The valley that led into the canyon where Comrade Crimson's cave was located was strewn with cherry trees, their branches reaching up to the blue of the sky. Rubies dotted the space between the sapphire leaves. She picked the cherries and ate them with delight. Life, Rosa thought. Fresh life, borne out of the goodness of this earth. When will this war end?

Rosa was never one to be swayed by a man's looks or demeanor. She was not a romantic, everybody said, but she felt a twitch in her heart when she met Comrade Crimson. Even though he had been wounded during a German air raid, he held himself upright, his arm bandaged across his chest. His eyes were clear and blue, his face wide and bright, and he smiled and said, "Comrade Rosa, it is my great honor to meet you. I am glad to see you are alive and well. I've heard of your many skills. Soldiers across the land say you're the greatest deer huntress that ever lived in these parts." Rosa smiled and blushed as she handed the message to Comrade Crimson and offered him a handful of fresh cherries.

In the evening, around the fire, they spoke of the national liberation struggle, the fight against fascism, the excellent work of the Partisans, and of the great need to create an independent new country when the war was finally won. The cave had a fresh water spring inside it, from which the soldiers drank. Some of them occasionally left the cave to make a radio connection. Rosa slept by the fire, along with the rest of the soldiers, and Comrade Crimson snored lightly in the night. Rosa left the following day, her heart full of promise.

She returned to the south, where Italian soldiers captured her during her next mission. She was sent to a women's concentration camp and spent a year of hunger and hardship that she preferred not to talk about. If Mona asked her about the camp, for she was curious, Rosa would just shake her head and say, "People say that bad people are animals, but animals are simple. They don't wage wars, they don't torture each other like we do. Humanity needs a great deal of effort to become simple, like animals." And she'd go quiet.

Rosa was released together with the rest of the camp in 1944, some months after the Italian capitulation. She was thin, hungry, and weak. She headed for the hills, to the forests, and for two weeks Rosa ate what she hunted and slept in the trees like she used to, until she regained some strength. When she returned she was attached to a brigade for a while, and fought on the front lines of one of the country's highest mountains, and took part in diversions and actions. This was where Ruben had also fought, in a different brigade. As the war drew to its close, and it became clear that Comrade Crimson would become the President, Rosa found her way back into the town she had left four years earlier. She and her brigade entered the liberated city on horseback, welcomed by a crowd of people who threw carnations at them. It was 1945; Rosa was twenty-three years old. Songs accompanied their entry, songs that the entire Nation would know and sing, all the way to Mona's times, and beyond:

A young Partisan woman threw bombs, hey!
A young Partisan woman threw bombs, hey!
Let it be heard, across the world,
That a young Partisan woman threw bombs!
Let it be heard, hey, let it be known,
That a young Partisan woman threw bombs!
And:
Forests, woods, a great thanks be to you,
You are where freedom was born,
You are where we got our liberation,
Our small and brave peoples.
Cannons are shooting in the forests,
And stars are dancing in the sky.
A young Partisan went into the forest,
Spilled his blood for his people.

Ruben was also entering town on horseback, somewhere behind Rosa.

Chapter 14

RUBEN ALSO JOINED the Partisans in 1941. He was unwilling to leave the three-year-old Diogen without proper care, but the things he had seen in the town and had heard of in the villages—the local collaborators gathering people and shooting them randomly, or sending them to concentration camps—appalled him. In the area where the Germans ruled, people talked of the occupiers killing one hundred locals for every German soldier killed. So finally, at the news that a Partisan fighter had shouted "Death to fascism, freedom to the people" before being executed by a local guard, Ruben decided that the time had come to join the liberation struggle. "It is either that or starve and die, or be shot and die," he said to himself. "And I owe it to the future generations in this country." So he left his little brother with the elderly aunt who had received them after they arrived from the village, and Ruben headed for the mountains, where he had been told he could report and volunteer. Right before he left, he watched Diogen, who was busy playing with pieces of wood at the time and paid no attention to the weeping Ruben.

Ruben's was a brigade of some fifty clueless soldiers with no more than a dozen rifles between them. Those who had learned to fight in the Spanish Civil War, and who had experienced modern warfare, taught the rest to shoot. Ruben did not know how to use a gun, but he soon proved to be a great shot at targets, moving and still. Birds and rabbits were cut mid-dash across the sky or green field; the enemy soldiers turned from upright, dynamic life to a crashing lifeless mass. Ruben worked hard at killing enemy soldiers, so that their weapons could be removed and the Partisan forces armed. They used any weapons they could get their hands on, Ruben doing his best to shoot from as great a distance as possible and kill as many soldiers as he could, trying not to think what it meant to kill, for this was a battle between Good and Evil. And just as in the war, in his dreams above the President Shop Ruben would sometimes crawl through the night with an M24 Mauser rifle in his arms; he would crawl through the marshlands, under the baking sun, through the insect infested reeds, frogs leaping away or staring at him with their beady eyes, and he had the most microscopic vision of the details around him. He crawled and felt the uniform grate against his skin, the back of his neck and his head as hot as that baking ball of the sun itself, the ground cracked like the surface of his brain, breathing a humid heat, the endless lines arching off and leading nowhere and everywhere, and Ruben crawled and crawled eternally, it seemed, toward a dead soldier, whose gun he had to get, and all the while the President's image was in his head, death to fascism, freedom to the people, death to fascism, freedom to the people, the town executions that he had witnessed merging with the landscape, crawling, crawling, the shooting of the man in front of his wife and child, the town square full of people, no one uttering a word, the man screaming death to fascism, freedom to the people, his arms up in the air, Ruben's breath punched out of his gut with the sound of the machine gun with which the man was executed, his body reverberating under the bullets. Ruben saw it all in slow motion, nothing existed in the same way after that moment, that first life that was taken with such speed, so easily, and then so many, and finally Ruben reached for the gun, the M24 Mauser, or was it the Karabiner 98k, or the Beretta submachine gun, he tries to feel the weapon but hears Rosa say, "Wake up, wake up, you're dreaming of it again," and Ruben would start, and sit up in bed, and nothing would make sense.

Later, the Partisans' weapons came from the Soviets and the British, the PPSh-41 and the Sten MKII. They were good guns, everyone thought, though when Ruben talked about it now, Diogen always said, "No gun is a good gun." Both Ruben and Rosa would answer, "To beat a fascist or a Nazi, the only way is a gun."

Ruben fought in the many mountains and forests across the country, and each time the Partisans were not defeated, they emerged from battle with more weapons, and as news of their victory spread, more young people would join their ranks. In the moments between skirmishes and sieges, the soldiers rested, ate the little food they had, read, and discussed the communist ideology of Marx, the urgency of defeating fascist forces, and of creating a new, just, and class-free society. Ruben took part in five of the seven major offensives, in which the Partisans were attacked and managed to escape. Rosa had passed messages for the commanders throughout these times, and later, when Ruben met Rosa, he said, "I cannot believe that I am holding Comrade Rosa in my arms, this is beyond all belief. We used to hear stories of your incredible survival skills. Someone once said you'd hidden from the Germans in a cave full of bears. Is it true?" Rosa said, "Of course not, who can hide in a cave full of bears? Nothing but fantasies."

But the truth was that Rosa had spent a night in a cave during a heavy battle in which there was a monsoon of bombs. She'd dashed into the cave and curled up in fear, thinking, Dear God in Heaven, can you see this? Dear Mary, can you see this? Jesus, Moses, anyone, can you see this? Make it stop if you can. And when the bombs stopped and all was silent and Rosa could get up to leave the cave, she lit a match to see where she was going, for she had hidden in the cave in such a panic that she was now entirely disoriented in the darkness and she lit a match and saw that there was a hibernating bear very near to where she had been curled up, the two curled up together, and she found her way out and was surprised how deep into the cave she had gone. She tiptoed out and rubbed her eyes for a long time because she could not see, and when she thought she could see she saw lots of red blotches everywhere, and carried on rubbing her eyes, and finally she realized that the red blotches were all her dead comrades, their brains around them like galaxies, like aureolae, their limbs strewn away from the rest of them, the whole scene like a surrealist painting, and Rosa stood there for a long time, and then a man came, one of the survivors who had also taken shelter somewhere.

"Where were you?" he said.

"In that cave."

"That cave is full of bears."

Rosa nodded, and that's how the story of Comrade Rosa surviving a cave full of bears came about, but Rosa remembered that day as the day her faith in God had been dislodged, or really, her faith in life, in somehow the ultimate good of man. If there is goodness then how can we be doing this to each other, how can God let it happen, she thought.

And she had asked Ruben when they first met, "How do you explain this?"

Ruben had said, "I don't believe in God. I believe in man, in his ability to choose right from wrong."

And thus it was that Ruben believed in the President as the man who led the country to fight against evil, and the man who managed to unite the people, who would often choose wrong over right, to see goodness, recognize it, and fight for it. And fight they did. The Fourth Offensive saw the Partisans retreat across the frozen mountains and lose their limbs and toes to hypothermia, as seen on the film that Mona and all the children of her generation saw on television in the days when the Nation was already well established. The Seventh Offensive was the final one, in which the Germans tried to eliminate Comrade Crimson, and failed.

Ruben's brigade, like most of the Partisan brigades, was made up of people from all over the country and from all walks of life; men and women, people whom he had never had a chance to meet before, and who displayed the kind of courage and solidarity that Ruben had never seen before, and would never witness again. Each battle was choreographed, danced carefully around the death that stretched between the Partisans and their enemy, and the soldiers moved in its shadows with an agility that, Ruben thought, could only be borne of an uncompromising striving for liberty. The Partisans pushed through the dense thicket of the forest, impossibly found cover in the open fields, waded through marshlands and blizzards, shot a billion bullets. They protected each other, bandaged each other's wounds, carried the wounded. They felt each other's hearts, and each death—and there were many—was felt by all. A young woman, shot in the stomach, died on Ruben's back as he carried her to the nearest field hospital. They washed in the snow, shared their meager food supplies, listened to each other's stories and memories of home and peacetime. In between battles, at night, they watched the sky with its cheerful, blinking stars, and Ruben thought of how the stars and the sky are always there, the immense space surrounding them a mystery, the space surrounding this planet upon which humans insist on pounding each other to death in ways that are amazing only in their relentlessness and innovation.

"If this war is ever over," someone asked on a quiet night as the brigade rested under the stars for a brief period, "will people ever want to fight another war again?"

The worst thing that happened to Ruben was when he was cut off from his unit in battle. He was pursued by several German soldiers and ran and ran through forests and bushes, falling, rising, stumbling, all the way to a cliff's edge, where he had to jump to whatever was beneath and beneath was an open, barren field, like the surface of the moon. Ruben ran across the field and came upon a shepherdess with an enormous herd. The Germans were near. The only thing Ruben could do was to hide under a bulky ram and grab it by its legs so that it would remain on top of him. And somehow, as if by miracle, it worked.

The brigades received regular news of Comrade Crimson and the progress of the Partisans across the country. They met for updates and strategies, and Ruben realized that four years had passed in this state of warfare and he felt as if he had never lived any other kind of life. When the war was finally won, it was hard to imagine going back to a normal life. What is a normal life, Ruben thought. What does it mean to sit down for a meal or go for a walk? To have a job, to work? What does it mean to not face death every day? He could hardly remember.

When he next saw his brother, Diogen was a seven-year-old boy, wispy and red-haired, freckles on his nose from the sun. Diogen did not recognize Ruben because the one picture that the aunt kept showing the boy, so that he would not forget his brother, was of a mustachioed, healthy young man—Ruben in his prime. At the end of the war Ruben was emaciated from the several bouts of dysentery he had suffered and the general lack of food. He looked so spent it was hard to tell his age. The boy stiffened before this man who approached him and grabbed him in an embrace that meant his face was pressed against the man's rough, stinking uniform. The uniform heaved and shook. His brother was weeping.

Chapter 15

THE NATION'S COLLECTIVE mind, like the mind of all other nations, was often occupied with the threat of a war. This was a Cold War, that's what everyone called it. Although the Nation was not involved entirely in this Cold War, it was not immune to the possibility of it, since it meant the possible annihilation of entire surfaces of the Earth, so powerful were the weapons involved. So when the order came for fallout shelters to become part of all new structures, the Nation was both alarmed and relieved. Alarmed because there was a threat of the world being blown up, or if not immediately blown up, the threat of the mushroom smoke of radiation loomed large, like in the pictures of Hiroshima and Nagasaki, things that no one in the Nation had witnessed in real life, but that sat imprinted in everyone's mind through endless photographs. The smoke mushroom, the poison, something clever scientists, the rulers of reason, Diogen commented, invented and then used it to destroy life and all its forms, and children were born with deformities for decades after, and of course no one wanted that, no one, so the Nation was relieved that the President was doing something to protect them, giving them shelters, and the tools for knowing what to do.

The Nation was doing everything to be prepared on all levels. At school, children older then twelve had a subject called National Defense and Protection. The textbook had the outline of the Nation's borders on its cover, the shape of which Mona thought looked like a shotgun, or a human heart, or a lung, depending on which way one turned the book. And inside the borders was the Nation's flag, with the beautiful red star in the middle.

The textbook covered mainly the topic of weaponry: the different types of pistols, shotguns, machine guns, cannons; how they are dismantled and put together again; provided detailed illustrations of what each part was called; the firing and range possibilities of all these firearms. One machine gun, for example, that Mona studied was the M53. Page 56 read: "It is an almost exact copy of the M42, produced during World War II in Germany and used by the Germans. The M42 was captured during the war by the Partisans, and then reproduced in the Nation's arms factories as the M53, with some minor differences. The aiming range of the M53 is two thousand meters, and the terminal range of the bullet is five thousand meters, though it is advisable not to aim at live targets from a distance greater than eight hundred meters, since the bullets disperse at that distance and the precision of the bullets becomes imperfect. Upon pressing the trigger, the firing pin strikes the primer of the round. This causes an explosion in the casing of the round, and the force pushes the projectile from its seated location."

Mona considered how one hundred to one hundred and fifty bullets per minute could be fired from the M53 and each bullet would cross five kilometers in search of something to receive it—a tree, a deer's soft muscle, a wall, a child's liver, the air itself. And at the end of its reception, unless the bullet just exhausted itself and fell to the ground, a wound, or death.

Mona wondered if she could fire a gun at a live target, at something warm, at a beating heart that pumped blood, a person, over there, an enemy.

"Yeah, of course I'd do it," a boy said.

Another boy said, "I'd be scared."

A girl said, "Oof, I hope it never happens."

Another girl said, "It's men who do it, no?"

"Well, my grandma was one of the main couriers and fighters in the national liberation struggle," said another boy. "She was better than my granddad at throwing bombs, everyone says, but my granddad disagrees. And my mother has to go to the emergency training sessions every month for Civilian Protection, in case of nuclear warfare, which, as far as I can tell, is highly possible. My father has a whole stack of tins of meat and sardines downstairs, he says that if the world is about to end, he doesn't want to go hungry like he did when he was a kid, in the war."

Rosa also attended Civilian Protection practice every month. Aside from the danger of a nuclear attack, the Nation had seen horrific earthquakes in the south of the country earlier on that year, which destroyed an entire city and the surrounding area, and the President had ordered that each citizen be proficient in first aid and other forms of self protection and organization, that the people should be well rehearsed in case of a natural or nuclear catastrophe. So the citizens were trained in putting out all kinds of fires, building tents and other temporary shelters, and well versed in working out the procedures in the case of limited evacuation of populations. The Nation rehearsed the so-called ABC Defense, which stood for Atomic, Biological, or Chemical weapons, which took shape in the form of creating an orderly structure of priorities—women, children, and the elderly first, men after—and precautionary measures, such as the even distribution of first aid kits, blankets, and packaged foods. The men were trained by the military for the event of a nuclear attack with the command "atomic right," which the commanders would shout at any given moment. The men, upon hearing the command, were to throw themselves to their left side immediately, since the army brass believed that throwing oneself on the floor in the opposite direction of a nuclear explosion would somehow shield the men. Sometimes, if Ruben was being particularly obstinate about one thing or another, Rosa would shout "atomic right" in jest, and Ruben, although aware of the joke, would say, "Rosa, you should recall the story of the boy who cried wolf and how no one came to his rescue." Diogen would roll his eyes.

There was also a period in which the Nation was in danger of being invaded in the north, some fifteen years after it had been formed. There was turmoil in the whole world, the East and the West, the Left and the Right, and the Nation stood in the middle, attached to almost no one. Or at least, mostly see-sawing between the two sides as it saw fit. The Nation created alliances with the former colonies of Africa and Asia, now newly liberated, collaborating independently, all under the clever guidance of the President. But then the neighboring countries were invaded by one of the giants and the Nation found itself preparing for the same. Ruben was mobilized immediately and sent to the northern border to dig trenches. He was exhausted by the thought of a possible new war, and returned, three weeks later, tired and aware that his strength, although still present in his firm body, was no longer what it was when he was young. He hoped with all his heart that he would not be called up to fight again, and that there would not be another war.

A small army bag was hung on the door handle in preparation for one of the women's Civil Protection sessions, when it was Rosa's turn for training. Rosa also took to hanging her gas mask on the door handle. Mona would stand in front of it, examining this disembodied, suspended grimace. It was a mask like those African masks Mona had seen in books; the African masks depicted either emotions or animals or symbolized something of the human part of nature to be used in a ritual or a dance or hung on a wall. This mask was a war mask, though she couldn't work out if it was a life mask or a death mask. It hid the face and the respiratory system of a person who was in danger of dying a nasty death if the mask was not worn or was removed.

The breathing noise of the mask, when it was attached to a face, through the round wire mesh tube, sounded like the breathing of the Elephant Man, a film Mona had seen and that had given her a unique trauma regarding human cruelty. Sometimes she would put it on in front of a mirror, and her face would get all hot with the vapor of her breath, and she would watch herself transformed into a thing, her body still familiar, but her features erased by a dark, blank stare. Or she would simply stand in front of the mask, her eyes and the goggles on the same level, and the mask would watch her darkly, not demanding anything of her, but always bearing the promise of a tragedy, of a removal from the world, a time when the air one breathes, the air that fills the lungs and the blood cells, would be unsafe. And not just for us, for all air-depending creatures on Earth, thought Mona. What would we do then? All that air that was produced by the lindens, the pines, the cedars, all that air would be gone, replaced by the great big mushroom of poison. A sense of panic and anxiety would grip her, and she would run to her bed and bury herself under the duvet. Rosa would pick up her bag of supplies and the gas mask and walk down the stairs, the suspended dark face swinging from her arm.

Chapter 16

MONA LEARNED ABOUT the President and the Nation from Ruben; Rosa spoke little of it. And then there was Diogen. When they were alone, Diogen would say things like: "Forget authority. It's made to put you down and make you small. Don't listen to any of them, be a real woman, know your power, Mona." But Mona had little grasp of what he meant. That morning, she had gone to the library and found the book *Tips for Girls*. There were all kinds of tips; Mona found a quiet corner and read with care. She looked for entries about how to kiss for the first time and how to know if you are a lesbian.

Mona and her best friend Maia used to play Adults together. They would sit with their legs crossed, holding cigarette chewing gum between their fingers like they'd seen their mothers do. They sat like that, pouted, sucked on the pretend cigarettes, stirred coffee cups that hovered in mid air, and said things like: Oh dear; you won't believe what she said to me; no, he didn't; oh my; what a cheek! Mona would show the new perfume she'd bought and spray Maia with thin air. They were as serious as possible. Inevitably the boys would come and shoot them down with their stick machine guns, driving off in their cars, which the girls only knew were cars because they made that revving noise with their mouths, dust rising in their wake.

But this was an old game. Her and Maia rarely played it now, only in moments when their childhood selves emerged. Lately, Mona had felt more confused more often; her body had started doing new things, things she did not want it to do. Her armpits stank at the most unexpected times; her breasts, previously the same as the boys' had started to swell and ache. She had hair growing in places where it had not grown before. All of it felt odd, out of control, and she had no idea when it would stop. It didn't help that her parents' friends would see her and say, "Oh, you're turning into a little lady, aren't you!" and Mona would blush and hate them.

Most of all, it was her feelings that confused her. Lately, she would break out in a sweat, her heart beating fast when Maia's older sister, the beautiful and indomitable Clarice (she had given herself that name, her real name was Jovanka), appeared. Clarice named herself after a Brazilian author, Maia told her, that Jovanka—as she was still known at the time—had come across on someone's book shelf. She styled herself in the author's image, apparently, adorning herself with beads, painting her nails, her eyes lined into almond-shaped magnets, smoking cigarettes and wearing clothes she had sewn for herself so that they were like the author's. In Mona's eyes, Clarice was enchantment itself. She was eighteen years old, a world away from Maia and herself—they had recently turned fourteen. Clarice held the promise of womanhood; when she flicked her hair, smoked with painted lips, the way she moved, the confidence, the confidence! Clarice also had progressive thoughts about the revolution, in tune with those that were being discussed at the student protests; although Mona could not fully grasp what they meant, the ideas that the students—or rather,

Clarice—talked about made more sense to her than her father's. When the students said "Down with the Red Bourgeoisie," it was clear they were referring to the communist elites, living in luxury. "This goes against the very fabric of the communist ideal," said Clarice, "against everything that our parents fought for, the classless society, the equality, the questioning of our values." Mona was enchanted.

When Mona visited Maia at home, she longed to be able to see through walls, into Clarice's room, imagining her sitting intensely over a piece of paper, writing her revolutionary novel, as she had told them she was doing when she sat down on a cypress branch with them, smoking a cigarette.

"My novel will break all the rules, just like Clarice's did," she said, exhaling the smoke upward, through crimson lips, gazing at the clouds as if she was reading the future for them.

"Have you ever tried reading the Brazilian author?" Mona asked Maia.

"I have. I didn't understand any of it. Clarice says I am too young to get it."

Mona tries it. Clarice Lispector. *The Passion According to G.H.* She finds the book in the library, sits on the floor, and goes to page one. "I'm searching, I'm searching. I'm trying to understand. Trying to give what I've lived to somebody else and I don't know to whom, but I don't want to keep what I lived." Even though she does not understand the text, reading it makes Mona feel closer to Clarice. Closer, without having to actually be close. She hates the effect Clarice has on her when she's near; the pounding of her heart, the dry throat, the nothingness of herself, knowing she is invisible to her except as her younger sister's friend, the pull of her gaze onto Clarice's body, its shape a woman's shape, and Mona's own limbs so skinny and long and straight and her body thin like an adder's. The protruding breasts felt unwelcome, she was not looking forward to their fuller form, and she felt she understood Clarice Lispector when she wrote "I don't trust what happened to me." Mona doesn't trust what happens to her, constantly.

She used to think that Ruben's words and Rosa's organization were her stable ground; also that the President's image protected her. Since Rosa lost the baby, the little baby boy, lost him to sleep—went to pick him up one day and he just wasn't breathing—Rosa mainly ordered things and watered the plants. When Mona saw the image of the Virgin Mary at her grandmother's house, she recognized Rosa's face in it, in the months following the baby's death. He is with God now, said grandmother, and Rosa just shook her head. There was talk of God's mysterious ways. Mona had been six years old. There were no more babies after that.

She did not understand if she fit into the picture of the order that had been presented to her; man—woman—child; school—university—marriage—child. She saw Clarice and she felt dizzy; she saw boys and felt nothing at all. She could not speak to her mother about it, felt ashamed to speak to her of such things, of bodily things, and matters of the heart.

Perhaps only when she was curled up like a fetus in the warm uterus of her duvet, did Mona feel an inkling of order. Only then did the body feel like it fit somewhere safe and familiar.

Chapter 17

DIOGEN SPENT THE morning trying to fight off the wasp nest of his thoughts: angry, boiling, stinging, relentless. He had walked home from the station finding more of the handwritten notes, only to discover when he arrived home that his room had been occupied by Great Uncle Robinson and that a large oil-drenched machine occupied most of the room.

"What on earth is this?" he yelped.

Rosa and Ruben explained that Robinson had become too old to look after himself so that he was now living with the family. Robinson was reclining in an armchair, mid-snooze, his wooly hat firmly on his head. He stirred awake when he heard Diogen's exasperated yowl.

"We are trying to make him move The Invention to the shelter but he can't go down the stairs easily and it's the only thing that gives him some joy," Rosa said.

"Have you seen the notices all over town?" Diogen said.

Rosa and Ruben looked at each other; they had not. Robinson had sneaked out at the crack of dawn—his hip was not too bad that day—and stuck up the notices from the train station all the way to the house. He'd come up with the idea of The Museum of the Future, which he thought ingenious, for it had imbedded in it an appeal to the tourists who arrived in town from the station, as well as the local folk.

"He's asking 500 dinars!" said Diogen.

Robinson looked sheepish, though an air of defiance suddenly washed over him and he exclaimed, "You are all too stupid to understand its potential!"

He walked into his room, slamming the door behind him. Rosa and Ruben shook their heads and went around town ripping down as many of the notices as they could find. They had been written in Robinson's unsteady, old-fashioned hand. He was indeed offering local produce in addition to the experience of The Invention, though he had not specified what the produce entailed.

Diogen's feet reflected his disquiet. After the shock that met him at home in the form of Robinson, he went to the river, hoping that he might bump into Ivan Ivanovich on the way. He walked down Ivan's street and past the place he knew Ivan went to for his morning coffee. Ivan was in the face of every seated patron, he was every man walking down the street. Diogen walked back to the river, hoping to be calmed by its murmur. Ivan's body was a sparkle on the water or a curl of a wave. Diogen saw him swimming across. He gasped, made a step toward the cliff's edge. It was December, it was impossible, of course. He knew that Ivan would never swim in December.

He walked up the hill that overlooked the town, hiked up the steep cobbled streets to the east; his thighs were only slightly strained, for he had worked hard at the Youth Action and felt fit. He crossed the big road that cut between the town and the hillside and moved up the gravelly soil. The beauty of this hill was that once you were at the top, you could walk a little down the other side and not see the city at all. It's why Diogen liked it. Pine trees and oaks and bushes grew here, and shepherds and shepherdesses sat on the ground with their herds scattered around them like fluffy clouds. Diogen had a good pace, kicking the gravel before him as he walked. The air felt fresh on his face and in his lungs, and he thought, What do I care for love, for Ivan, for any of it? He sang. A song of cherry blossoms and snow falling on them, a spring song. It was winter but he wanted to feel that spring was on its way. His voice flew across space, followed by silence. A wind blew. He looked back, the town sparkled under the white sunlight like a galaxy; the river slithered through the valley. The further up he got, the colder the air, until it felt like his ears were being slashed by the gusts of wind. Snow gripped the rocks; as the sun hit the snow, it crackled like a fire, and dripped.

Diogen walked toward a shepherdess reclining on the ground. She had spread out a plastic sheet, then a blanket, and covered herself with a sheepskin rug. She rose as he approached her.

"Don't get up," he said.

She sat up. "Oh I'm so glad to see someone, anyone," said the woman.

"It's so peaceful here."

"Hm," said the woman, looking around. "You find it peaceful. I think it's fucking boring."

The old woman's hair was wild, her mouth a gap. She looked at him and picked up a rock from a pile she had gathered before her. She threw one of the rocks at the sheep.

"I hate these motherfuckers," she said. "All day, every day, herding them, running after them. They scatter in all directions and you don't know which way to go. I wish they'd all die."

She threw more rocks and made the *prrrr* sound that is used to summon sheep. Diogen just stood there.

"Whatever you do every day, in the same way, you come to hate it," said the woman, lying back down. "Even the lover you once had. You think the sun shines out his ass, but he becomes boring if you live with him every day."

She hissed at the sheep and closed her eyes.

Diogen carried on across the green field. He kept turning around at the sight of the old woman.

Did she really happen? What is happening to me? My whole world is disintegrating!

He walked down the hill in a hurry.

Chapter 18

IVAN HAD SEEN Diogen that morning. He had stood at his window and stepped away. Diogen's copper hair was slicked back like the wave of the sea against the setting sun, the brown searching eyes, hands in pockets, wide strides. He knew where Diogen was going, and he knew that if he wanted to find him, he'd be at the riverbank. He turned and caught a glimpse of himself in the mirror. The uniform clung to him like unfamiliar armor, a stiff olive wool with lapels that almost reached the shoulders. He started to undress slowly, and removed the uniform piece by piece, folding the trousers, vest, jacket, as he had been taught in the army. The red star was always to face up. The blue, white, and red of the flag too. Nothing should cover them.

Ivan had returned for the weekend, after a month away in the barracks. He was in the artillery unit, and the first month had been all about learning the rules, singing the anthem for the flag, and training. The other soldiers were each stifled by their own homesickness and the mundane nature of the extreme routine. Several enjoyed the formulaic life; they found comfort in the repetitive duties, some said they almost felt purified by the daily hard physical exercise. Some were depressed by it, and sat smoking at night alone in the dark outside. The superiors were harsh and superior, as Ivan had expected. He felt as if his insides were clenched by the metal jaws of a bear trap. But he knew that he had to endure, for there were another eleven months ahead of him.

"Coffee is ready," he heard his mother say through the door.

"Coming," he said.

The fire burned in the stove and everything was in its place. He noticed a new picture of the President on the wall.

"Where's that from?" he asked.

"Ah, I walked past the President Shop, went in to say hello to the family, and then I saw this picture. Isn't it lovely?'

Ivan nodded. "How are they?"

"Oh, very well. The younger brother was at the Youth Action. Ruben said it would be good for him, now that his military service is coming up."

"Yes?"

"It's true. He's quite unprepared for that sort of thing, that much is clear. He's always in some dream world, humming to himself, fishing at the river. Well, you know him. You know how he'll fare in the army."

Ivan said nothing.

"They said they are having a welcome back party for him, and that maybe you could go over, speak to him about life in the army. Say something positive about it. He's apparently very afraid to go."

Ivan nodded as a current went through his body at the thought. Diogen's slightly hooked nose, his strong lips, the freckles that the spring sun coaxed out on his face and on his arms and shoulders. Ivan remembered that Diogen had freckles on his elbows, that once, as Diogen was showing him a particular spot where wild strawberries grew, he caught a glimpse of Diogen's freckly elbow as his arm bent and brought the fragrant strawberry up to Ivan. He shook off the memory.

"When are you meeting Milena?"

"In half an hour."

"You have to choose a ring, my dear, it won't choose itself. The poor girl is desperate to see it."

Ivan said yes and got up. Slightly irritated. He knocked over the coffee cup and apologized.

"Groom's nerves," his mother said and wiped the spilled coffee with a red, white, and blue tea towel. "Don't you worry, it will all be all right, you'll see."

He went to his room, picked up his cello, and felt it for a while, its familiar form comforting in his hands. He played, twenty-five minutes exactly, and then the doorbell rang.

"Hello, Milena, my darling," he heard his mother say. "Come in, he's right here, playing his music, you know him, haha, what a dreamer he is, our Ivan. Ivaaan! Milena is here!"

His heart sank. He put the cello away and walked to the door with concrete feet.

Milena had glistening straight hair the color of the night sky, and eyes full of light.

"Shall we go?" she said shyly when Ivan appeared.

They went. Ivan in his navy coat, and Milena in a crimson one, and he put his hand on her shoulder as they walked down the street to the jeweler's.

"It's such a beautiful day," said Milena.

Ivan nodded, realizing that he forgot to ask his mother what time the party was at the President Shop. A simultaneous sense of turbulence and delight filled his gut as he remembered Diogen's face and the perfume of a wild strawberry on a January morning.

Chapter 19

"WHY AREN'T YOU here? Oh, why aren't you here?" Diogen sang as he walked down the hill, his voice gliding through the air. "When new wildflowers are adorned with the pearls of midnight, my chest swells up with desire, oh why aren't you here, before me?"

He looked at the town beneath him. He loved it, he hated it. It was his home, he had no place there. Only the river, only the river was without conflict for him, and as soon as he thought of the river he remembered Ivan and his beautiful face, his coal hair that looked like granite in the sun, each hair a sparkling galaxy. All Diogen wanted was to bury his face in Ivan's hair and breathe. He would even eat that hair, he thought, and he couldn't bear to think of his lips upon Ivan's without almost doubling over with pain, those corals upon his face that he would never part from.

"A bluebell peeks out from under a dew drop, a fragrance sings from the blossoming tree, but to me all is sorrow, a whine and pain and tears." He finished the song and then said, "Oh dear God, I have to go to the army on top of it all."

The truth was that Diogen had tried everything he could, after finishing his degree, to get out of serving in the army; tried claiming insanity, being unfit, you name it. Nothing had worked. Partly, Diogen suspected, because Ruben had told the officers who'd examined him that Diogen was trying to get out of his duty, that there was nothing wrong with him. He hated Ruben for it.

"I know you saved me, brother," he had told him, "and that had it not been for you, I'd not have lived. But I breathed and survived because I wanted to be free, not to serve in some stupid army, following orders like an idiot!"

Ruben was exasperated. "Every man in this country has to serve, if he can. It's our duty. Don't you see? If we were to be attacked tomorrow..."

"Attacked? Who is going to attack us? We don't need anyone to attack us from the outside. Look, it's already happening here, in this bloody shop that is like some temple to that man," Diogen shouted, pointing wildly to the President's pictures. "We, in this temple, are attacking each other!"

Ruben shut his eyes, trying to block out his younger brother's blasphemous ingratitude.

"You're attacking me, I'm attacking you, we don't need an army, we can just kill each other here, right now!"

Ruben opened his eyes and stared at Diogen in shock. "Kill each other? Whatever for? What do you mean, dear brother?"

"I want to be free! To breathe as I like, to live my life as I want to. Not to spend an entire year obeying absurd orders. Left! Right! Stand! Sit! Like a dog!"

Diogen seemed to be on the brink of tears.

"But it trains you. It forms you. It disciplines you. It teaches you to learn that you can't do as you like, not always, mostly not, life isn't like that," said Ruben just as Rosa walked in. "We should always be grateful for what we have."

"Not that shit again," Diogen said under his breath, for his love for his brother stopped him from swearing directly at him.

Diogen threw Ruben a glance so frustrated and lost and alone that Ruben's heart broke in an instant. Diogen stormed away and slammed the door, and the next thing they could hear was loud singing from his room.

"He has never felt the unity of the people," Ruben said. "The loyalty and dedication to the cause of preserving our liberty."

Rosa said, "Can't you leave him alone, really," but she knew she was saying it to herself mostly.

Ruben shook his head. "Some creatures need to be broken in. He doesn't know what's good for him. Apart from any loftier ideals, he should serve, get a job, get married, have children. He doesn't know what's good for him."

Diogen's singing got louder. Rosa sighed and went into Mona's room. Mona was at school. Rosa sat on her bed. She had found a pack of cigarettes in Mona's drawer the day before, one had been smoked, and she'd also found a love letter to a Clarice, sealed with a lipstick kiss. Rosa remembered Ivana, a girl from her village, who was caught kissing Ana, and when word got out, both were beaten so badly by their fathers that they could not leave the house for a month. She knew that Ruben would not do such a thing, but she worried about her daughter.

Ruben had sat down on a chair in the living room, next to the gramophone, and put the needle on a record of the President's speeches. It was an early one, from the beginning of the republic. Its rhythm was staccato, at first, the President emphasizing every word: "Dear—Citizens—of—the—Republic." And then it went into a flowing discourse on the virtues of the Nation's Way. Rosa knew the words by heart. And she knew that Ruben was in need of calming down, for this was the speech he played to himself when he needed to breathe, breathe, breathe.

Rosa wondered what to do about Mona as she casually opened a desk drawer. She could not approach Ruben about it, and she couldn't talk to Diogen while he was in this state.

There was a diary in Mona's drawer. Rosa took it out and held it in her hands.

To open or not to open?

Chapter 20

MONA HAD BOUGHT a packet of cigarettes. She wanted to see if smoking was any good. It must have been, if Clarice was doing it.

Maia watched her. "You look ridiculous and it smells disgusting."

Mona puffed, and choked, coughed and coughed. Whose fresh healthy lungs embrace poison without resistance?

"You look like those five-year-old gypsy kids who smoke."

"Shut up, you're being racist," Mona said.

'You really don't look cool, plus your mom and dad are going to kill you."

Mona tried a few more puffs and crushed the cigarette against the soil. They were hiding in a bush.

"Not cool," said Maia.

"Yeah, okay, I get the point."

"Why do you even want to smoke?"

Mona shrugged; of course she couldn't say. To impress your sister, she would have said, and that would have sent Maia into shock, she was pretty sure. She had also written Clarice a letter, declaring something like her love. I love everything about you, she had written, your lipstick, your nails, most of all your soul. I also love the name you gave to yourself. Rosa, having found it inside Mona's diary, had read it and smiled, and also her heart felt heavy at the prospect of her daughter's heartbreak, or longing, all the confusion coming to her, the years of confusion, the getting, the not getting, the wanting what you want, then getting it, then not wanting it any longer.

Dear Fluffy, I tried smoking today. It was kind of cool. Disgusting too. I want to do something that Clarice does, so that we can maybe do something together; I think if I smoke with her, I won't appear so young to her, so irrelevant.

Diogen came in and sat on Mona's bed, next to Rosa. Rosa hid the diary behind her back. This had become his room too now that Robinson had occupied his; a mattress had been packed in for Diogen. The walls of Mona's room were a patchwork of posters of hair metal bands: men with perms and leather jackets and Vaselined lips. Some sported electric guitars with sharp, wild edges. Lots of stickers, from when Mona was little: bits of Snow White scattered, several dwarves, in pieces, a tiny foot, a nose, a beard.

Rosa checked the time. There was another half an hour before Mona returned.

"Ruben has some big news to announce at your party. He's been invited to the President's boat, on a three-week tour of the islands," Rosa said.

Diogen looked up. "Really? With the President himself?"

Rosa nodded. She opened Mona's drawer and pointed to the cigarettes and the letter. "She's infatuated with a girl."

Chapter 21

THE DAY ROBINSON had invited Mona to be the first witness to the greatness of The Invention, the machine consumed so much power that the entire apartment, together with several others on the floors above and below them, short-circuited, and it took electricians three days to get the system working again. So Mona had not seen into the future. After Diogen had found the notices for a visit to the Museum of the Future hung all over town, The Invention was moved to the shelter, where Mona now spent time whenever she got a chance.

There had been a shelter Cleaning Action the previous week, and she had participated. This had given her the opportunity to surprise herself with her ability for deviant behavior—one of the keys, which only the adults were in possession of, had been left unattended. So she took it and went to make two copies of it for herself, replacing the original key without anyone noticing. She told the old man who cut the keys that they were for the community locker. She had gone out of the neighborhood to prevent the possibility of being recognized and having to answer uncomfortable questions. Watching him, she remembered the President's original calling as a key cutter, which she had seen pictures of all her life in the President Shop. The large iron wheel scraped the metal and promised the opening of a door that for Mona held a place where she could spend undisturbed hours; the tree was no longer right, it was too exposed. And there were too many kids around. She intended to offer the second key to Clarice, as a way of offering a secret to her. Maybe you can write there, she'd tell her. She wanted to show Clarice that she was different, that she dared do things that others didn't. They could smoke there, and talk. It would be cool.

"Shelters against atomic or hydrogen bombs are nothing but coffins and tombs prepared in advance," Diogen shouted at Ruben, after the Cleaning Action had finished. "The minister said so himself, I don't know if you bother to listen."

"Well, you can stay outside if there is an explosion, brother, you're quite welcome!"

During the Cleaning Action, one of the neighbors had spoken of a rumor that a shelter had been made just for the President and his inner circle, a long tunnel dug into a nearby mountain. It was speculated that it was ten kilometers long, had all the newest radio technology, an area for tanks and weapons, even a place to keep two airplanes, should the President need to make a quick escape.

"Apparently, there is a luxury area for the President and his wife, with a four-poster bed and a record player. They even have all the President's records lined up. His favorite is Miles Davis."

"Nonsense!" said Ruben. "Why do people listen to all this nonsense? Miles Davis! The President never speaks of this kind of thing."

But, at night, when covered by the cloak of sleep, Ruben dreamed of the President's bunker, its mouth hidden in a rock face, opening onto a tall, cavernous hall behind a sealed heavy door, as if to an underground castle. Ruben, for some reason dressed in an astronaut's suit, levitated through the long neon-lit corridors, from one room to another. There were various rooms, of various sizes, containing only red telephones and relief maps of the country hanging on the walls; there were rooms with small televisions, the President's face delivering a speech that Ruben knew; another room with television screens, a white flurry of snow on them. An enormous space with a single airplane in it. A kitchen with a food taster, a man responsible for monitoring both the quality and vitality of the President's food; he was, as a real servant of the Nation, ready to die first, were the President's food poisoned. But in reality, he was simply getting more rotund. This man, Ruben knew, had been picked from reality, since Ruben was aware of the existence of such a person in the President's inner circle. And then Ruben walked into the President's private quarters, finding the President's wife sprawled out in a four poster bed in a cream-colored negligee, her hair in a dark beehive, listening to Miles Davis. The President wasn't anywhere to be seen, and the wife, upon seeing Ruben, sat up lazily, her legs and shoulders bare, and said to Ruben in a voice as soft as honey: "Get out of that moon suit and come to bed." Ruben, delighted, obeyed.

He awoke with a start, his heart thumping, and to his great shock and self disgust, he was aroused by a desire as powerful as a nuclear reactor. Rosa was asleep. He dared not wake her or try to make love to her. He thought it would be dishonest, given what he had just dreamed, though, of course, he knew he could not be held responsible for his dreams. He got up, went downstairs in his bathrobe, took the key to the shelter, and descended the stairs. There, he unlocked the safe, took out the golden bust of the President, and started to clean it with the special cloth, trying to set his thoughts straight and remove the lascivious images of the voluptuous President's wife that kept flashing before his eyes.

Chapter 22

ROSA HAD MANY rituals. She woke at exactly the same time every day, washed her face and hands and her body, wiping each part with a warm flannel cloth, her armpits, under her breasts, between her legs, her legs, feet, and then she put cream on her skin and brushed her hair. She made coffee, prepared breakfast for everyone. She opened up the shop. And on Thursday mornings, for she had chosen this day as the first day she left the house after baby Yasen died, she went into the woods. No matter the weather. Yasen was born three years after Mona, a strong baby, eyes like blue marbles, a mouth as soft as the inside of a cloud. Rosa still wondered what had happened. He'd looked perfectly healthy. But one day, he simply did not wake up. His life sucked out of him overnight. In his crib, unmoving. Rosa had seen death, all kinds of death, had caused death, had been at the brink of death, but she had never experienced such short life, which just the day before had felt so forcefully evident in the tiny grip of its fist, the ferocity of its cry, she had never seen such life just disappear. There had always been a cause: war, hunger, savagery, disease, old age, accidents. But what was this? God's will? The wheel of Fortune? Bad luck?

After Yasen's death, Rosa spent a month in bed. There was nowhere she could go, no one she could talk to, nothing she could do. Ruben was devastated, and could do no more than hug his wife and weep. It was Diogen who helped her.

After the month in bed, Diogen went into her room and said, "Rosa, this cannot go on. You have to get up. You have another child. She needs you. You've been through the war, you know how to fight." Diogen said whatever he could think of, hoping it might stir the light in her soul. "I am taking you to the forest."

He dragged her out of bed, took a warm flannel cloth and wiped her body. Face, breasts, between her legs, legs, feet. Every morning. It was as if she was being embalmed, or had returned to being an infant herself. Rosa surrendered to the process, felt herself removed from her body, like the flannel was wiping a wooden board that was somehow now meant to be her body. There was no sensitivity to her skin, no tickles, no pain, no sensuality. Then Diogen would put her in the car and drive out of town, to the mountain where the forest changed from short, shrubby trees to tall birches and oaks and beeches, and the shade was comfortable and the light dappled and golden. The forest emerged onto a deep canyon with a sparkling river below, and at the top of the mountain was a bench and a shrine to a goddess who was said to bridge life and the afterlife and where people went and left mementos for their deceased loved ones. Diogen knew that Rosa would at least be stirred by the forest, and it was true that when she entered the woods Rosa felt as if some of her had returned, that she had caught a glimpse of a way out from the deep grief that had entombed her soul. Every day she and Diogen would go up to the top, and she would sit at the shrine, which was on a fresh water spring, and weep for her boy, thus suspended, Rosa, Comrade Rosa, the great huntress and warrior, between life and death, between the soil and the sky. And no amount of war, she thought, of that collective battle of life against death, was equal to this, a grief that was unique to her. Ruben had dedicated himself to work, closed himself up in the shop, talked to no one of his loss. Rosa wept and prayed to the goddess that her son would be in a safe place, and her heart healed, slowly, as much as it could.

Mona got her mother back, and Rosa sometimes took the girl up with her, but mostly she went alone. She preferred the woods and the shrine to the graveyard, the emerging water from the spring giving Rosa some sense of a continuation of life, of a nurturing liquid coming from beyond, from the Earth's very core, coming out and going back beyond, and only in that way could Rosa fathom the mystery of the randomness of life and death and an order beyond the grasp of the human mind.

Chapter 23

DEAR CITIZEN,

As an exemplary citizen of our Nation, you are cordially invited to spend three weeks traveling around the country's islands with the President, aboard his ship, The Blue Dolphin. *During this time, we will be engaged in hearing lectures from the President, and understanding the future concerns that face us. We will examine how to keep our nation strong.*

Ruben put the letter down. This was more than he had ever dared dream of, though dream of it he did, occasionally. *The Blue Dolphin*! Three weeks! He did not know what to do with himself. Today he was desperate again, having to announce this news at the party for Diogen, who seemed determined to ruin everything Ruben stood for, everything the President stood for. Ruben had called a military commander he knew, and told him that he should not relieve Diogen of his army service any longer, under any circumstances. He had a twinge of doubt as he was saying this into the telephone and the commander kept repeating "yes" in a tinny voice, with Ruben feeling that the commander was doing something else as they talked and possibly not really listening, but Ruben felt that his hesitation was mere weakness on his own part, and that really what Diogen needed was a year of enforced discipline, which Ruben had obviously failed to give him, possibly because Ruben felt he was on the brink of weakness and peril himself quite often, his heart giving way when he knew reason should prevail. Goals! Ruben had read a book called *The Psychology of Success* and tried to implement the title in his life.

"What kind of success are we talking about here?" Rosa had asked when she saw him reading the book.

"The success of truth above lies, of order over chaos. A person must be focused on his goals, must be passionate about how they live their life and always keep focused. All this you see around you, none of this would have been possible without focus. Yours, mine, the President's, all of the people involved."

If Diogen had been around when this was discussed, he would've hissed, "For you success is a pathology."

Ruben felt that Diogen could not be left to go around wandering in the unfocused state that he seemed to live in, like a bug bobbing inside a ball of gelatin, upon the waters of the world, and the gelatin would soon solidify, in Ruben's opinion, and Diogen would become one of those insects trapped inside amber or glass, God forbid. Ruben shook himself to get rid of the thought. He needs to be removed from there with a sharp shock and a pair of precise tweezers, he thought.

"He's unfocused, you see, that's the real problem," he told the commander. "He needs the iron hand of the military service." Ruben had shouted the last part.

"Yes," said the commander.

"The military has the best tools for making a man out of him," he roared into the telephone receiver.

"Yes," said the commander. "We will do our best, as we do with all our young men. Only, you know, sometimes these guys really don't want to be there, or they are really unfit. Last week one cut himself with glass, all over. He smashed a glass and took the pieces and cut himself. He'd done it once before and then he did it again. We had to release him. They'll do all sorts nowadays to get out. Times are changing, the spirit of protecting the country isn't as strong as it once was."

Ruben gulped and took a breath to say something, then stopped.

"I don't know what material your brother is made of," said the commander, still talking as if out of a tin.

Ruben could not release the image of this career military man sitting in a small sardine tin, with a micro telephone in his hand, and the thought was distracting. Ruben struggled to concentrate on what he was saying.

"But basically, the iron hand of the military service either makes you or breaks you."

Ruben had heard of this young man the commander mentioned, and several other such cases. It was a year; it was tough. Up at the crack of dawn, and every possible kind of discipline imagined was exercised upon them, plus the kind of rough treatment that went with the service. Ruben had enjoyed it, and yes, he had served in the days when being in the military was considered an honor, not only considered an honor, it was experienced as an honor. But as the commander said, things were changing. Chaos was seeping into order, Ruben felt, and the straight line that he had walked in order to get to where he was now standing—moreover, where he would be standing soon aboard *The Blue Dolphin*—was all thanks to that straight line of order, the clear values that were projected to the nation, that every individual, had they followed it, could count on to lead them to a warm hearth, a happy family, a clear mind.

This was what Ruben's thoughts went over and over again, first doubt then certainty, then doubt again, especially at night, severe doubt, avalanches of doubt at night, when the bruised darkness descended upon the world and his sleeping wife produced breathing sounds that were deep and safe and she was elsewhere and Ruben felt alone in their matrimonial bed, and the President's picture would somehow start to glow in the dark, his teeth would shine, the whites of his eyes, his smile, and only that would calm Ruben and usher him into the warm embrace of sleep. In the morning he was steady in certainty again, at least for a while, if he had not had one of his dreams, nightmares rather, of eating live bugs, cockroaches, or crickets, of lifting the struggling insect to his mouth, feeling part delighted part horrified, and crunching into the soft center of the body through the crust of the bug's protective shield, and as he chewed and swallowed, the wiggly legs of the creature would tickle his insides and Ruben would wake up with a start, reaching to Rosa, but finding her gone. Lately, she was often gone from bed, and Ruben would put his head on her pillow and breathe in and try to regain that balance of certainty. Is it Diogen I am crunching, he would wonder, before washing away those thoughts with a cold shower.

Rosa woke at dawn, to watch the edge of night and day. She wondered how Diogen would survive the army. One never knows with him, she thought. He could still somehow get out of it. Though she knew that Ruben had called the commander. She had thought about removing the pack of cigarettes from Mona's drawer, thus subtly letting her know that she had seen them and taken them away, but was giving her a chance to improve herself. But then Diogen had said that Mona would just hide them somewhere else and at least this way she would be able to monitor what was happening with Mona without pushing her away. She had started having the same dreams that she'd had after Mona was born, of losing her, of leaving her in a shop and forgetting about her and coming home and realizing she had left her, and she would wake up startled, the bedroom a cold dark cave around her. Sometimes she dreamed of the boy, of his little body while he was still alive and his breath warm and his muscles full of life, and then sometimes that dream would go further, to when she picked him up from the cot, that morning, and she would find herself surrounded by bears in a cave, and it was wartime again, and Rosa would wake with a start, soaked with sweat. She would get up and go look at Mona sleeping, her dreams fading away slowly. She would study her daughter, who was now a mystery, a process, her thoughts and activities hidden from Rosa. She watched her for a while, listened to her breathe, her hair an auburn filigree upon her face. Rosa always heard Diogen wake up, for Diogen always woke at dawn and took a brisk walk to the river, where he practiced some movements he had devised for himself, part dance, part martial arts, part cardio. He had a large, purple book of yoga positions called *Yoga Every Day* that Mira, the town hippie, had brought from the capital, and which Diogen had borrowed. He chose some yoga positions and mixed them in with karate strikes, and several dance moves. He decided to do this routine at his secret river spot because he needed more space than was available in the flat, especially since losing his room to Robinson, plus the moves involved jumping and grunting and even something akin to a chant. He also believed that breathing in the clear morning air was optimal for getting the maximum benefit from any exercise. Mona found him one day staring at a lit candle and upon asking him what he was doing, heard something about the third eye and opening that by sitting and focusing on the candle's flame. He told her to try it. Mona had sat down and stared until her eyes watered, but she felt no third eye opening.

Diogen practiced his movements in solitude because there he was shielded from the curiosity of others. He had learned to be careful about exposing his differences to the world when some boys, upon seeing him sing and dance by himself in the street, as Diogen was prone to doing as a boy, losing a sense of where he was, showered him with rocks and curses and he ran and ran as far and fast as he could. This is how he found the hidden spot by the river; the boys had chased him, and when he turned the corner behind the large mosque down the gravel path, he ran into the bushes that seemed to encase him, like a catacomb. He sat there and could see the boys looking for him, but they seemed blind when they faced the bushes. The only other person to have found the hidden spot without guidance was a young man who'd said his name was the Roma word for "lament." Diogen was surprised to find someone in his secret spot, but the young man immediately said, "Hey, I also like to hide, I hope you don't mind me joining you." He said he could find the perfect place to hide within five minutes of entering any town and that this was pretty much one of the few perfect hiding spots in town. Diogen sat next to him. Lament was semi supine, one leg resting on the other, smoking and chewing a piece of straw simultaneously. He produced a bottle of homemade plum brandy. The two of them drank from it. Diogen felt like he was drinking petrol, but he also enjoyed the burning in his chest that seemed to extinguish the other burning, the burning of his heart, for he had just had an argument with Ruben about one thing or another, and the flame of his anger was being devoured by ethanol fire.

"What are you hiding from?" Diogen said.

"The iron fists of my father, the flames of our caravan, which I set on fire with a lighter I found, that's when I was little. The police, for stealing, the big guys who were looking for me because I bailed on my wedding. Many things. You?"

"I hide from the President and his remote pair of eyes."

Lament laughed and patted Diogen on the back.

Lament came for five days, every day, always at 7:00pm, as the curtains of dusk descended upon the mountain-ridged sky. It was summer. Diogen was seventeen years old, Lament, Diogen thought, between seventeen and fifty. It was hard to tell, and he would not say.

"What does it matter, how old I am? Old enough to know I need to hide."

Lament spoke in a way that was at times tender, fragile, his voice like a soft humming of a river, almost hushed. That's when he spoke the truths of his heart. Other times, when he recalled his adventures in a way that sounded like a movie to Diogen, Lament would adopt a louder voice, and start speaking out of the corner of his mouth, like a gangster. Lament also liked to sing, songs that were new to Diogen, he'd not heard them before, or perhaps he had, but not sung in the way that Lament sang them, and Diogen would sit, heart and mind soaked in brandy, and Lament would sing, and Diogen felt his heart held in the invisible hands of the song, the beauty of his voice like the delicate light of a firefly. It was also with Lament that Diogen first made love. Diogen had sung a song for Lament, his eyes closed the whole time, his voice going through a variety of warbles, soars, and gentle lows and as he finished, Lament's hot brandy lips burned a stamp on Diogen's, and Diogen felt a heavenly and infernal joy, knowing that in order to live where he was, he would have to destroy his nature; and if he was to survive in his heart, he would have to nurture it.

As the two young men lay naked in the shelter of the bush that night Lament said, "We have just committed the original sin."

They laughed. Diogen felt as if they were the first men on this planet, and there was no Ruben, no President, no military service, nothing at all except the river and the sky and the protective verdant womb that held them. And then Lament never came back again, though Diogen had waited at the spot for days afterward, hoping that perhaps he would. There was no ache in his heart.

It was after Lament that Diogen met Ivan. And it was the way that Ivan received the wild strawberries that one time, when Diogen had fed them to him, that turned his heart into a crater full of spiking hot lava, and infested his mind with chaos.

Chapter 24

THE WELCOME BACK, Comrade party started with the National Anthem being played off the record player. Ruben had an ancient record player with a horn speaker, "like in the movies," he often said, and he insisted the National Anthem be played off it every time. He stood by the old machine with his hand over his heart, a glimmer of a tear in his eyes. He was always emotional when it came to the National Anthem, but today he was particularly sensitive. Ruben was disconcerted by a dream he'd had.

It was thirty years into the future, and he was living in another country, a Western country. There had been a war in his homeland and he was an immigrant, an artist of sorts. The President had died, or had been exiled—he was not the president any longer, in any case. Ruben was aware of all of this in his dream, but it had been announced to him that the President had returned, as if from the dead, and it was Ruben's job to organize his welcome back party, a large festival, at an enormous hall. Ruben was running around putting the program together, gathering the artists, managing everything. He saw the President and went to sit with him, but instead of the luminous, smiling, strong man he knew, the old man before him was bloated and rancid, unhappy about returning to this position, demanding to know who'd called him back. When Ruben went to answer, the President would just shake his head and not listen. The last thing Ruben remembered before waking up was the President in full uniform, standing on the stage, utterly bitter and miserable.

Ruben started the day panting and sweating. Could there be war in the country, again? Could the Nation disintegrate, the values of Brotherhood and Unity evaporate into thin air? Could the President's message die, his image die? He could not bear to think of it. He knew of the disagreements, battles, wars of the past. He knew that there were people who did not like the order of things as they stood in the Nation. He knew there was an island, far out in the sea and bare like a bald head and lacerated by wind and sun all year round, where those who disagreed publicly with the order of the Nation were sent to rethink their ideas. He knew there had been an attempt on the President's life in the West, by a resident group of emigrants from the Nation, who thought the President was the devil incarnate. But didn't every nation have its divisions, its problems, just like a family? He could not shake off the dream the entire morning.

Chapter 25

ROSA ATE A sandwich and read:

Pinned,
onto midnight,
the moon is a silver pendant.

She enjoyed reading haiku for its neatness. Haiku had become a very popular import from Japan, along with *ikebana* arrangements; several of Rosa's friends attended courses. Even Rosa went to one, and Mona remembered the green spongy square that served as a deposit for the flowers. But Rosa passed on the ikebana trend; she preferred plants, watching them grow. She had just completed three hours of reshelving all the products in the shop, dusting them and arranging in what she thought was a more ordered order. Ruben walked in.

"Wonderful ordering, Rosa. I am, as always, proud and delighted to be your husband. We now need to start getting things ready for the party."

The President Shop, along with other stores, occupied the ground floor of a building called The Corner, a structure that was built around a large corner, and considered something of an architectural feat at the time. It was a concrete pyramid shot through with long balconies in straight lines that proclaimed simplicity and order. The living spaces faced southwest, so that light penetrated the simple square rooms through large openings. The tenants had enough privacy while also being able to spy on each other through the geometric shapes that were cut into the balcony dividers.

For the party, the shop filled with the tenants' community, like Boris and Ana Pavlovic and their two children, Mak and Anya, who lived on the first floor. On their front door, like on every other door in the country, the patriarch's name was inscribed. These nameplates were usually a metallic rectangle, which could be gold or silver colored, but some people personalized it to reflect their individuality. So Boris, being a painter, had his name etched in metal the shape of an artist's palette. He wore a beard and black turtlenecks. His wife wore flowery skirts that went no further up than the knees. Their children were withdrawn. If you peeked inside their kitchen through the window, when no one was around, you could see Boris's easel through the door of his studio, left ajar so that the smell of the oil paints could evaporate; apples in an acacia bowl, the wood's grain swirling along the cupped shape like a whirlwind; the washing up, done and dripping, and a floral tea towel stretched and drying on the sink. Ana had been reading, and left the book face down, the open pages embracing the plastic tablecloth beneath them, surrendered to their pause. The scent of their home was that of Boris and the paints and alcohol; Ana's rose perfume and silence; and the children's secret affairs, played out and suspended under the acrylic blanket stretched over the armchairs, forming a hidden chamber. Boris often went out drinking with Zoran, from the third floor; Zoran and his family were admiring the many photographs of the President.

Plates and glasses and cutlery sometimes came flying from Zoran's windows, like spittle from a raging mouth. If shouting was heard from their flat, most of the neighbors walked in a loop, for there had been times when household objects landed on the heads of people walking underneath Zoran's windows. There was a smell of violence in that apartment, of *rakija* and the stench of urine and toxic sweat. The morning light was dappled and dancing on the doors of the wooden wardrobe in their bedroom, the bed bore the imprints of their heads, from Zoran's nightmares of being chased down a dark alley in nothing but underpants.

Dragan Gavranov, from the fourth floor, stood in conversation with Ruben. He was a remarkable and productive member of society, didn't drink, and helped everyone outside his home. But in the bedroom he would push his wife against the wall and punch her, for he did not trust her and was convinced that she loved all men but him, despite his good deeds beyond the walls of their home. Zoran and Dragan would meet on the stairs, on the landing, and greet each other, and their wives would greet each other, and a silence enveloped their bruises.

Vlatko Rakov, who had retired from engineering and dedicated himself to framing pictures after suffering a stroke, occupied the ground floor. Ruben gave him photographs and paintings to frame, and he was standing with Zoran's wife, explaining how the framing process worked. Zoran's wife, Gordana, was nodding her head vigorously. Vlatko tried to spend each day involved with the process of framing, and moving aside the anxious thoughts about the past, his mother, his dead wife, and what his life had been, or might have been. With each cutting of a piece of wood, or plastic, or whatever the frame at hand called for, Vlatko pushed away the memory of his chance to move to Frankfurt with Dana, who was now a grandmother to three, apparently. He knew because an old acquaintance of theirs had come round to have a frame made last week and told him all about Dana and how he'd met her in the street on one of her visits, and how she was still glowing despite her years—sixty-five, the acquaintance had said with astonishment, sixty-five—and Vlatko felt his stomach churn, for his memory of her was from their youth, just after the war. She was radiant and smiling and he used to call her "my apple" for she had such ruddiness in her cheeks. But when his mother heard that he wanted to leave the country to go to Germany with her, to work there, she fell ill, fell on her deathbed, which she kept falling onto at even an inkling of bad news, so that Vlatko could never leave her side.

Maia and Clarice's parents were there, and Maia had come, and Mona and she stood together; Clarice was at some school activity.

"Is Jovana coming?" Rosa asked when she came to offer drinks off a tray to the family.

Mona's heart beat a little faster; Rosa gave her a quick glance as she waited for their response.

"Yes," the mother said. "I think so, she said she would come and say hello. But she's in a world of her own nowadays. You know what they're like when they hit puberty. God knows what goes on in their heads."

"She's got it into her head that she's going to be a writer," said Clarice's father, who was president of the local engineering company and a man who believed that nothing one could not see existed. "As if that ever earned anyone any money!"

They all laughed, except Mona.

Ruben had joined them during this conversation and added, "Of course, she could write about the President, that is always respectable and well paid, and you have a permanent position inside the President's writers' group."

That irritated Mona and suddenly she felt Diogen's ire become hers. Always with the President, whatever the topic, the President, even the President would be sick of the President if he had to hang out with Ruben! She excused herself, walking away, toward the stock room, to the toilet. She walked past Robinson, who was snoozing in a chair. He suddenly opened his eyes as if he had sniffed Mona passing.

"Psst! Hey! When will you take me to the shelter?"

"Soon, Robinson, soon. Tomorrow?" she said.

Robinson nodded and went back into his snooze. What Mona did not know was that Robinson had also made a copy of the keys to the shelter and had set about working on his machine in the hours between 4:00 and 6:00am, moving relatively lightly down the stairs. He had kept up the front of the fragile legs for the sake of the family and to ward off suspicion.

Mona stood in front of the mirror, the green blue wall behind her, a light bulb above her, bare and jaundiced. She examined her face: almond eyes, the color of freshly turned earth; hair, rich, auburn, somewhat of a wavy mess; freckles, which she always had an issue with. She'd been called Pippi Longstocking by everyone who lacked imagination regarding girls with freckles, which also de-sexualized her, she thought. How can Clarice ever think Pippi Longstocking is cool? Lips, good. Sexy. Sexy? She pulled up her shirt: small breasts. Something like apricots in their first incarnation, post bloom. Maia's breasts were already three times the size of hers. Already the boys wanted all the slow dances with her so that they could squeeze up against her chest; Maia was unaware of this and unsure of what the breasts meant in the new world surrounding her. But Mona had heard the boys talk about it, and they were crude. She was skinny, too, which was not good, she felt.

The party was going on outside. She remembered when she was smaller, when parties would go on and the parents weren't looking, she would take a toy to the bathroom, lock herself in, and experience the loveliest sensation when sitting on her toy. The boys talked about this at school, gathering together to masturbate, they called it, revealing all kinds of details about pornography, always harsh, always masculine. The girls never said a word, either to each other or to the boys, even though one day, Natasha, the most sexually advanced girl in their year, had found her parents' video cassette with pornography on it, and they stuck it in the VCR and watched, a group of them, Maia too, but she left after a minute feeling a sense of shame and confusion, the scenes of enormous genitals on the screen both traumatizing and arousing. For Mona, sticking her fingers in her underwear was a way to lose herself for a few minutes, a way to relax in a tense moment, and here she was, in the bathroom, watching herself in the mirror and climaxing and seeing a swirl of colors, sometimes the images of pornographic genitals flying in front of her eyes despite herself.

She returned to the party and Maia said, "Where have you been? Everyone's here, your uncle's drunk. There's going to be a scene, I can feel it."

Clarice had turned up. She sat in a corner, talking to Ivan. She wore a polka dot dress, a minidress, even though it was midwinter, her curly hair with a thick fringe, lips made up in purple, the gap in her teeth that Mona loved so much it ached. Clarice leaned back in the chair, touched her hair, laughed, threw her head back, laughed some more, fixed Ivan with her eyes narrowed. Mona had never seen Clarice at a party, talking to a man. Her insides were being gored with a burning hook.

Rosa carried various drinks around and watched Mona watching Clarice, kept her eye on Diogen. He'd arrived steaming drunk with Nikolai the hunter, both with blood-shot eyes, Nikolai with the dogs, who went around sniffing everyone, and Ruben getting nervous, going quite crazy inside, really, but Diogen didn't care. Somehow, between walking in the hills and coming into town, Diogen had come across Nikolai, and between them they finished a bottle of brandy. Nikolai was fond of Diogen, felt him to be otherworldly; he was also suspected in town to be the murderer of dogs. He lived near the river and dead street dogs were often found at dawn under his window. He had an air rifle and hated dogs, except his two hunting dogs. The rest, he said, stank. There was a story that he had been in a concentration camp as a youth, in World War II, and the guards would always come with barking dogs to beat the prisoners and that's why he hated dogs and killed them. But he loved Diogen, always said, "If only there were more people like you in this town," although Diogen never understood why, and if today Nikolai was to share his brandy with Diogen then so be it. Who was Diogen to say no, he reasoned, although he knew that the party was that afternoon, and that Ruben had big news and that it all had to be at least reasonably presentable, but in the end he didn't care.

"Oh dear brother man, how am I ever going to escape that military service, eh?" Diogen said to Nikolai as they made their way to the President Shop.

"I don't know, but you'll find it shit. The army's no good for anybody with an ounce of brain and self discipline, and I've seen you practice your moves every day at the river, and I say what beautiful moves, you don't need the army, plus you wouldn't be able to do that there in the morning. Everyone would think you're a faggot and kick your ass."

Diogen laughed and said, "Oh but I am, I am."

Nikolai laughed too, both of them mindless with alcohol, Diogen leaning in and saying, "Say Nikolai, did you shoot Boris's dog, Boris from the first floor, was it you?"

Nikolai laughed more and said, "You should have seen it, ran off faster than a Lamborghini."

When he walked in, Diogen did not see Ivan. Ivan, who had spent the day buying an engagement ring, nauseous, yet stoical, felt that talking to the sixteen-year-old girl at this gathering was the most he was capable of at that moment. Rosa grabbed Diogen by the arm, discreetly, she thought, and pulled him into the bathroom, splashing his face with water.

"Honestly, you really know how to make a storm out of a breeze," she said.

Diogen looked at her and said, "A breeze? I'd rather call it a wind. And are we talking wind, wind?" He giggled.

"Just be quiet out there."

When they went back out, there was no improvement in Diogen's state. Then he saw Ivan.

Chapter 26

RUBEN HAD DECIDED to go ahead with the plan, never mind drunken Diogen and Nikolai and the dogs, and the fact that Robinson had come to life all of a sudden, telling Nikolai all about The Invention and the Museum of the Future and how Ruben was repressing his genius, saying, "You must come down, brother, and see it, you'll have to pay of course, I intend to die a rich man," and Nikolai was laughing like a bear and saying, "Yes, yes, I'd love to, maybe I can even buy this Invention of yours," and Robinson saying, "Never, never! But maybe we can work together."

"Ladies and gentlemen," Ruben now announced, hushing up the various conversations and waving his hand in the direction of Diogen, who stood in the middle of the room, unsteady on his feet, Rosa by his side. "This party has been organized to welcome back my younger brother, and to simultaneously say goodbye to him. He has just completed his time at the Youth Action, spending his energy to help the Nation be built out of the ashes. As we all know, this is a great honor and a delight."

The tenants clapped, briefly, confused at the sight of Diogen looking so drunk.

"My brother is also to commence his military service in two weeks, which is another great honor."

Another round of applause sounded and Diogen sat down on a nearby chair, turning pale, the room spinning around him.

Robinson made a farting noise with his mouth and said, "That'll be a laugh!"

Ruben ignored him and continued. "I unfortunately will not be here to see him leave, because, ladies and gentlemen, I have been invited to join our dear President on board of his ship, *The Blue Dolphin*, for three weeks, to accompany the President on a tour of our country's greatest islands."

A grand round of applause erupted at this point and Ruben performed his piece de resistance of the evening—in a single fluid motion, he pulled the moss green cloth off the glass case containing the golden bust of the President, the statue lit by the spotlight. He joined in the applause, applauding himself, tears filling his eyes. He had practiced this move for an hour before the party, so that it went smoothly, and smoothly it did go. Ruben was happy. Robinson, who had fallen asleep again, was startled. The dogs barked, and Diogen, his nausea reaching its peak with great velocity, vomited onto the floor voluminously. The women gasped. The dogs, delighted, ran up to Diogen and started licking the steaming, stinking pools.

Some of the guests started to leave, others rushed around to get cloths to help clean up the mess.

Ruben shouted at Nikolai, "Get these bloody dogs out of here."

Nikolai, laughing, cooed, "Come on little ones, that's not dinner."

He led the animals by their collars out of the shop. The dogs resisted, but finally walked out into the cold night.

Clarice was doubled over with laughter.

"Stop laughing and get up," her father said and went up to Ruben to shake his hand, saying, "Congratulations, comrade." He gathered up his family, taking Maia by the hand, and left.

Ruben went up to Ivan, who was stuck to his spot, and who seemed like the most sensible young person around, and said, "Could you please take him out for a walk, he needs to get some fresh air. If you don't take him out, I think I might kill him."

Ivan nodded, took Diogen under the arm, and said, "Come on, let's have a little walk."

Diogen obeyed, like a little child, hearing Ruben talk about cleaning up the mess.

The President's golden statue stopped glowing; Ruben had turned off the spotlight.

Chapter 27

DIOGEN WAS SHIVERING. His mouth tasted of brandy and vomit. And yet, as luck would sometimes have it in the midst of misfortune, he now had what he'd been dreaming of for months—Ivan's arm under his. Though he was, admittedly, hanging off it in the most unbecoming way.

"Sorry, man," he slurred.

"It's okay."

They walked. Diogen noted they were walking toward Ivan's house. He said nothing, let himself be led by Ivan, who soon took the keys out of his pocket, unlocked the door with his beautiful long fingers.

"I'll make you some coffee," he said, pushing the door open. "Your brother is pretty pissed off. I don't think you should go back until you're sober."

Diogen nodded.

They entered the empty house. Ivan opened the door to his room, turned on the light, and took off his shoes.

"Wait here."

Diogen lay down, nodding, obedient. Ivan went to the kitchen, put the water to boil, and took out the coffee. Diogen struggled to keep his eyes open, his head pounding, thinking, Ivan's bed! I'm in Ivan's bed! He let out a gurgle of delight and fell asleep. He dreamed of Lament. Lament came to him as he rested on the floor in the bushes and said, "Wake up, here's coffee," and Diogen opened his eyes; Lament's face had never been more beautiful. There was sunlight in his eyes, and he smiled warmly, and Diogen closed his eyes again and felt Lament's lips upon his, soft and strong, and Diogen returned the kiss and felt his chest fill with light. He sunk again into the womb of sleep.

Ivan sat by the bed and read, waiting for Diogen to stir. He could not focus on the text. He watched Diogen's surrendered body, his face flushed and serene with that unique trust in the world when one is asleep. What beauty, he thought, in this man. And at that moment Diogen seemed to be having a nightmare, and in fact he was, he was being chased down a green field, where Diogen had been dancing freely, passing by Ruben, the President, and the commander, all dressed in military uniforms, and each had a set of cutlery in his hands and they were coming after him. Nikolai's dogs had turned up from somewhere too, and Diogen was convinced they were all chasing him to eat him up. He ran and ran, panting, struggling for his life, and the men and the dogs were coming closer, and just as the commander was about to stick his fork into him, he heard Ivan's voice—Ivan's voice!—Ivan's voice?—saying, "Wake up, you're dreaming."

Diogen opened his eyes and took several eternal moments to understand where he was; a room, unfamiliar, pictures on walls, night, and Ivan sitting by the bed, his hand on Diogen's shoulder. How on earth? He blinked, felt Ivan's hand withdraw, and grasped it. It was warm, Diogen's freezing; Diogen said something to that effect. He did not let the hand go, he could not.

"Thank you," he said.

Ivan nodded, said, "I made you some coffee," and liberated his hand from Diogen's. "Are you feeling any better?"

"I had a terrible nightmare. Some cannibals wanted to eat me."

Ivan laughed.

"What happened at the party?" He had a vague recollection of the statue, Ruben's speech, the dogs.

"Your brother announced that you were going to the army, that he was going on *The Blue Dolphin*, and then you vomited."

Diogen put his head down on the pillow. "I had better go back."

"Have your coffee," said Ivan. "You can sleep here, if you want. I can put a mattress on the floor for you." He said this last bit without intending to, surprising himself. "I mean, if you want, if you don't want to face your brother just yet." He felt his face go hot and tried to cool it down with the power of his rational brain.

Diogen was taken aback. Sleep on Ivan's floor? What had happened? Had the gods decided to simultaneously humiliate him, before annihilating him in the military service, but before that, had the gods decided to gift him the realization of his one, his greatest, desire—this man right here, who seemed to want Diogen to stay on his floor—was this what was going on? Was getting furiously drunk and making an unpleasant scene at the President Shop the way into heaven? Surprise, desire, joy, panic, shame—everything was happening to him at the same time and all he could produce in response to Ivan's offer was a small giggle. He sat up on the bed and took the coffee cup, his hands quite unsteady. What he really wanted to do was sit in Ivan's lap, like a little child, and be cradled, and he wondered about this impulse. Was it a regression to a mother he had never really had the chance to meet?

"You know, my brother raised me," he started, not knowing where he was going or why. "He was my mother and my father, he was everything. When I was a baby, he saved my life. He carried me across a freezing mountain to the town doctor. You've probably heard the story, everyone here knows it."

Ivan nodded. "I know something."

"But he himself had nobody to raise him. He was fifteen and started working and entered the orphan program to honor the President's life and work. And so the President raised him, the image of the President, his speeches, coming off a fucking record. And there he is, still serving. He built a life for all of us." He stopped and looked at Ivan. He was beautiful. "But I don't want that life." He saw Ivan's uniform, hanging up like a flat headless corpse. "I don't want the army. I don't want any of it. He loves the President, but he does not know the President. He knows me, and he knows I won't survive the army, a whole year there, I'll go mad."

Diogen began to cry, his head in his hands. Ivan, not knowing what to do, sat next to Diogen and put his arm over his shoulder, and Diogen wept on Ivan's chest. He felt pathetic, but at least he was pathetic on Ivan's chest, he thought.

When he calmed down, he said, "Can you play me something? Your favorite piece?"

Ivan, relieved to be able to take some action, got up, took the cello out of its case, and played. Diogen lay down again, closed his eyes, listened, opened them again, and watched Ivan play; in a kind of trance, Ivan played, his eyes closed, at times opening them and seeing Diogen on the bed watching him.

Diogen, feeling that the world's burdens were exclusively his, felt the world's burdens disappear when Ivan suddenly stopped playing, dropped the bow and followed an urge in his hands, which was of course the urge of his body. He took Diogen in his arms, cradling him like a child and kissing his hair. Diogen was sobbing again, and he thought that Ivan was too, though he did not know why, had no idea that Ivan had proposed to Milena that day, regretting it even before he had done it, although Milena was a lovely girl, but that there were no two ways about it, that his mother was expecting it, that she depended on this, on the possibility of a grandchild or two, she had said to him, that he was all she had, that her life otherwise had no meaning and that Ivan was in charge of providing that meaning. That the army, in his case, was a welcome escape from the marital duty he was expected to fulfill, that he could not wait to go back to the routine and the mindlessness of it, that the love letters he occasionally wrote to Milena were copied out of a book he'd found, mostly, the romantic parts, and that he had thought of Diogen while he was writing those letters, and was always trying to silence those thoughts and ignore them, thinking that perhaps the marriage to Milena would finally help him eventually, possibly, get over his thoughts of men instead of women, but here he was, with Diogen in his arms, and he wondered if he was taking advantage of the situation while Diogen was sick with a hangover in order to feel his body, for once, just once, and the sensation was so powerful he could not stop himself from weeping too, and he felt Diogen sit up on the bed and Ivan opened his eyes, thinking, Whatever happens, happens. Mother has gone to stay the night with Grandmother in the village.

Chapter 28

WHAT COULD IVAN do? When Diogen left his house at dawn, he put on his uniform and took the train. He was meant to stay home another day, but he couldn't face his mother, couldn't stomach the idea of Milena turning up. He and Diogen had said nothing when they parted. It was snowing, the morning was white: the sky was white, the air was white, the ground was white, his breath was white. He was glowing inside, felt Diogen's skin on his, his face on his. He'd never known such complete union with someone; yet he knew that was all there was, that there would be, could be, no more. And so, Ivan was immersed in the glow of their union on his train journey and as he approached his destination, he knew that he had to extinguish the sensation of Diogen from his being. It was no good going into the barracks with this softness in his gut.

Ivan went inside the barracks and signed in.

"You're back early, that never happens!" said the soldier who kept the checklist for returning soldiers. "What happened? They gave you hell at home?"

"Something like that."

The next morning, Ivan rose at 5:30am, with the rest of the cavalry unit. He went to wash his face, a towel hung around his neck, like a boxer. His entire being felt as if it had been soaked in suffering, flattened by agony, filled by pain then roasted in the oven of misery. There was not an inch of his self that was not wretched. He had thought that returning early and being away from Diogen would make the experience flake off slowly, yet steadily. Army life was so cold and hard, and the very opposite of Diogen's passionate hot embrace, that there was nothing there to remind him of it, thought Ivan, but God in heaven how wrong he was! Every man around him was Diogen; every muscle movement reminded him of Diogen, every groan of a stubbed toe or sound of restless sleep—it was all Diogen. Everything and everyone was Diogen, yet no one was Diogen and Ivan felt more alone than the Moon circling the Earth. On top of it all, thought Ivan, no one must know it, ever, no one must know the most beautiful thing I have ever lived and am likely to live.

He went to wash his face and brush his teeth. He leaned over the ceramic sink, saw his face in the mirror, saw Diogen's face.

"You come back one day early to get on the officer's good side, eh?"

He turned. One of the soldiers who was already around six months into his service was standing next to him, looking like he did not mean to be friendly. Ivan had just completed his first month of service. The men who had lived through the first three months took it as their duty to transfer the suffering inflicted upon them by soldiers who had arrived before them onto the freshly recruited soldiers. This man, standing next to Ivan, at 5:37, was evidently keen to offload some of his early morning misery.

"Eh?" Ivan said.

"Yeah, you think you'll get on the officer's good side by coming back early, you dick. Move over, let me wash."

"I'm using the sink, as you can see."

"I want to use it. Move over."

"You'll have to wait until I finish."

The man, who was bald and had a thick neck and a very round head, put his towel around Ivan's neck and pulled him back. Ivan, who had only been in a handful of fights in his life, and had always tried to avoid them if possible, saw a darkness cover his vision, and the sensation of suffering, which had previously populated his soul with such fervor, changed color and transformed into painful black anger. What could he do, he later said to himself, but punch the guy straight in the face, so that his nose turned into a crimson petunia, that South American plant Ivan remembered his father telling him about; his father who had been a keen gardener, had said that petunias were closely related to tobacco, cape gooseberries, tomatoes, deadly nightshades, potatoes, and chili peppers. "You'd never think it, by looking at them, would you?" Ivan had to agree, you wouldn't. So he punched the man straight in the nose, and the man's face was bleeding and Ivan's hand hurt and the man tried to fight more, but what the man had underestimated was that Ivan's punches had force and he was fast on his feet. Ivan regretted the violence after the tenderness, but welcomed it too, because it somehow gave him a break from feeling so miserable. More thoughts of his father came back to him at that moment, between the punches, and although everything took less than a couple of minutes, for the other soldiers came in and separated them, and then the officers came in and ordered them to get ready and find them in their offices, immediately, all of it took a short time, but Ivan's mind found the space to recall his father, his father telling him how their neighbor Ahmet, the man who had the most beautiful garden in town, a garden he had tended himself from start to finish, with a pebble path and a rose bed, the incredible dahlias that grew there—native to Mexico, his father said, all these crazy beautiful plants come from far away—the healing Arnica, cousin of the sunflower, the Artemisia, a common bush with the most enchanting smell, its name sharing the name with that large nuclear power plant, it had been written in a newspaper one day, "cherno-byl," anyway, how Ahmet's wife came home one day to find him hanging off a rope, dead as a doornail, his father had said, and they were all shocked, how could Ahmet do something like that to his wife, if he was going to hang himself. Why didn't he do it somewhere else, imagine the shock to her, and Ivan's father said "It's because Ahmet was gay, everyone knew it, he had married his wife and had children but his heart was never in it," and Ivan remembered all this as they pulled him off the round-headed man, whom he had punched it seemed more than once, they pulled him off like a bug waving its arms and legs, and both soldiers got the punishment of no release to go home on weekends or going out at night for three months, and they were to do all the dirty jobs in the barracks. For the next three months, Ivan and the thick-necked soldier were to load coal, take the rubbish to the dump, which was at least a kilometer away, clean the toilets, you name it. Ivan was glad for the exclusion from society, and the exhaustion. He was also glad he could not go home. With time, he thought, Diogen would be but a pale memory.

After a while, he and the thick-necked man made friends; they used the same cloth to clean the toilets and the cutlery of the exceptionally unfriendly officers.

Chapter 29

CLARICE WAS WALKING home from school, billowing dress, nails painted red. Mona stood in the shadows, waiting for her to pass. The day was crisp and radiant. As Clarice neared, Mona stepped out.

"Hey," she said.

Clarice stopped. "Oh, hey. You startled me. I was lost in thought. What's up?"

"What are you doing right now? Do you have somewhere you have to be?" Mona had rehearsed this first part of the speech.

"Erm, well, I was going home. Why?"

"I want to show you something."

"Okay," said Clarice, a little confused. "What?"

"Follow me," said Mona and started to walk toward the Corner. She was trying to stay steady, maintain an air of confidence. When they got to the entrance, she took the key for the shelter from her pants pocket and said, "We have to make sure no one sees us."

"You have a key?"

"Shhhh."

She unlocked the door and quickly glanced around. All clear. She motioned for Clarice to descend the stairs. She then locked the door behind them. The luminous sky disappeared behind the heavy door and their eyes were met with a darkness that one expects to find only inside a tomb.

Clarice grabbed Mona by the shoulder and said, "I can't see a thing."

"Don't worry," Mona said, pulling out a flashlight and lighting the stairs.

Mona had been down here earlier and put a couple of lamps inside, to make the place look nicer. She turned them on and they glowed like suspended balls of heat. The shelter was nothing but a concrete room, with benches lined against the walls. Blankets were folded and piled up in corners. Some reading material was stacked under the benches, like first aid handbooks, a dictionary of catastrophes, and the President's collected works, brought down by Ruben. There was also a botanical field guide, to help survivors identify different types of plants and trees, and one about spotting local birds, which Mona had been looking at.

"It's odd," she said, offering the botanical book to Clarice, "were there to be a catastrophe and we had to shelter here with gas masks on, this would probably be the most precious book."

Clarice leafed through the pages, but stopped to say, "What's that smell?" She looked around a bit more. "And what is that thing?"

She pointed to the Invention, which, covered by a sheet with orange flowers on it, looked like a beast, poised to leap. The machine stood in the far corner of the shelter.

"Oh, it's The Invention. Belongs to my batty great uncle, Robinson."

Clarice went up to The Invention and lifted the sheet—the machine glistened with thick oozing oil that puddled up all around it, as if it was alive and breathing. Clarice quickly dropped the sheet and stepped back.

"Creepy," she said.

"Apparently it can see into the future, but it takes too much power." Mona laughed. "As the future might. Can't expect to see into the future on a domestic electricity rate, can you?"

Clarice laughed.

"Want some tea?" Mona asked.

Mona had tried to make the shelter as comfortable as possible, both for herself to read in and hide, and, most importantly, to present to Clarice as an attractive option, notwithstanding the unforeseen element of The Invention's brooding presence, mostly felt through its potent odor. She had brought down her diary, which she deduced that her mother had been reading; she'd also stashed her cigarettes here and taught herself to smoke convincingly. Except for Ruben at the end of every day, no one had the inclination to descend into this cold subterranean space. She had no idea that Robinson made his pre-dawn escapades down here, and that he had noticed that Mona had made it into a secret nest. He thought he'd keep it to himself. Mona had also brought down a small heater. She turned it on. Gave a blanket to Clarice. She made peppermint tea in a tin pot. Clarice said nothing, just sat down on a bench with the blanket and watched Mona.

"So what's all this, you spend time here?"

"It's quiet, and no one ever comes. I make tea and read and smoke."

"You smoke?"

"Yes. Want one?" She took her pack from a box where she held the rest of her kit: her diary, spare light bulbs, gloves for when her hands got cold, tea bags.

"Does Maia smoke?"

"No. Just me."

Clarice took a cigarette and they lit up. Mona had picked up the demeanor and gestures by watching the adults and copying their moves. She was doing well, she thought. They sat in silence for a moment, waiting for the tea to brew.

"I have another key, if you want," Mona said. "I thought maybe you can read here, write too. You can bring your typewriter down. I don't have one, but I compose some poetry in my notebook."

Clarice said nothing for a while.

"Yeah," she then said. "It's not a bad spot."

Mona was delighted, but didn't show it.

"We could have a signal knock?" Mona asked.

They agreed that they would knock three-pause-two-pause-three times, to warn each other when they were coming in. If there was no knock and the door was being unlocked, they'd hide. They shook on it. Then, not finishing her tea, Clarice said she had to go. Mona gave her the key.

"Well, I'll let myself out," Clarice said with a smile.

She walked up the stairs thinking that Mona was odd, but that she also liked how daring she was.

"Thanks," she said as she left.

The next day, Clarice knocked three-pause-two-pause-three times and unlocked the door. Mona had been there since school finished, drinking tea and eating butter cookies. Clarice came down, lugging her typewriter. Mona helped her find a good spot for it on one of the desks. They would hide the typewriter under the blankets at the end of each session, they decided. Clarice was wearing a hooded jacket and a hat, her brown curls sticking out from under it. She also had fingerless gloves on, which Mona silently admired.

"What's your novel about?"

"Love. I'm trying to understand the mystery of love."

"Oh."

"Yes," said Clarice. "We are raised with this idea that a woman must find love and marry. That a woman can't taste love, in the physical sense, before marriage. Well, I say crap to that."

"Yeah."

"I've had sex, you know." Clarice was looking at the ceiling, made of rough cement. "I've had it several times. The first time, when I was thirteen. With my cousin's friend, in the village. We went to a bush and did it there. He was seventeen. He didn't know what he was doing, and neither did I. But I wanted to try it."

Mona swallowed. She was thirteen. She could not imagine herself being behind a bush with a boy and having sex. She felt hot. A great unease flooded over her. She glanced at The Invention, thought she'd seen the thing move with her unease. She looked away from it, said to herself, "Don't be silly."

"Men have so much more freedom than us. I'm telling you this because I think you're cool, you can obviously keep a secret if you've got a key to this place. I congratulate you on this, normally everyone just wants to know what everyone else is doing, but you're clearly a woman of private affairs," said Clarice.

A woman? thought Mona. Me?

"Have you had a boyfriend yet?"

"No," said Mona. "Not yet."

"You'll find men are not that impressive. But I'm looking for love, true love. That's why I'm writing this novel, to discover, if I can, what true love is about. I don't want to marry and spend my life tending to a husband, like my mother does. Clarice Lispector was an ambassador's wife. She was also an incredible writer, the best there was, in my opinion, but she spent so much of her life living as a wife. I really don't want that."

Mona felt she should say something. "Yeah, that would not be good."

"One guy, my dad's work colleague, used to come around to our house all the time. One day, when my dad had gone to the kitchen and I was standing in the living room, he put his hand inside my dress. I was surprised, and I wasn't. I wasn't a virgin anymore, but I didn't know if this would ever happen, I mean, I saw the way he'd been looking at me. I was fifteen, they like that, these older guys, they like us young girls."

Mona was shocked. "What did you do? Did you tell your dad?"

"No!" Clarice laughed. "I let him. Next time he came when my parents weren't home and we fucked in their bedroom. He taught me all I needed to know to be a good lover."

Mona blinked, looked at her shoes. They were black. And round. "Oh, wow," she said. Her throat was dry.

"You're shocked, you think I'm disgusting, right?" said Clarice, part mocking, part searching.

"No, no!" Mona sat up. "I think it's amazing, yeah, you should learn about this stuff."

She didn't know what she was saying, felt something she could not name.

"He came round all the time after that, sneaked out on his lunch break. I used to put on my mother's lingerie, her high heels. It was weird. It was like I was my mother, but not my mother. I used to wait for him to turn up, wearing nothing but lace underwear and high heels." She laughed. "It drove him wild. I liked to watch the way he got more and more needy for my body, for these roles I used to play for him. He asked me to slap him, to step on him with the heels, all sorts of shit turned him on."

She stopped, thought for a while. Mona was imagining Clarice's heel prodding the man's thigh; there was something comical about it.

"Then I got bored. Told him I'd tell my dad if he insisted, so he never tried again. Though I still see him circling around the building on his lunch break. Anyway, I should do some writing now." She turned around to her typewriter and bashed on the keys.

Mona went upstairs for lunch. Rosa had been cleaning out wardrobes, re-shelving books, sorting cupboards. Beef stew was on the table, around which Diogen, Ruben, Robinson, and Rosa sat, blowing into their heaped spoons. It was two days after the party. Mona felt lightheaded from Clarice's stories and the oil fumes that filled the shelter.

"How was everyone's day?" Rosa asked.

Diogen just nodded; he had not spoken for two days.

Ruben started talking about all the things he needed to prepare for his trip. "They say to bring warm clothing. The deck can be a rough place to stand on if it's windy."

Robinson said, "Today, I put two more pigeons on the path to recovery."

After The Invention had been moved down to the shelter, he had taken to pigeon keeping, constructing a large cage on the balcony out of bicycle wheel spokes and various other recycled metal materials. He now kept—and released, for their "wing exercise" as he called it—over fifty pigeons. The cage was enormous and took up most of the balcony. Robinson's rate of building was so prolific that the cage—which Ruben and Rosa and Diogen had agreed to after Robinson had lain on the bed half-dead for four days after The Invention had been moved downstairs, only going to the toilet but even that was done on his knees like a tortured martyr—went from a relatively small thing to an enormous dome construction in one afternoon.

"Really, uncle," Ruben said, "I wish you would stop with the pigeon keeping—the birds are shitting all over the balcony and everything stinks again. And it's impossible to sleep with all that goo-goo noise in the morning."

"What is it with you people?" said Robinson. "Can't I do anything to keep my soul alive? First you deny me my life's task by moving it into that catacomb, then you want to take my pigeons, which have become like my babies!"

He was about to enter into one of his dramas, so the family decided to keep quiet.

"Also," he said, "someone has been rummaging around my money again."

"No one is rummaging around your money, Robinson," said Rosa. "You have no money."

Robinson eyed everyone suspiciously and bit into a piece of beef. "Yeah, right," he said.

The sound of the gurgling pigeons came from the balcony in a great reverberating noise.

Mona didn't speak. She had nothing to contribute to this exchange, which was turning into a daily ritual. Her heart was heavy. It was as if an entire layer of the Earth had been peeled off by Clarice's confession, revealing an unbearably hot ground that she was meant to stand on. She had no idea whether the Clarice she loved and the Clarice she had spoken to were the same Clarice, and she didn't know if she wanted to talk to Clarice further, but something about the idea of her opening up like that, of sharing her secrets with Mona—and what secrets!—felt as if pulling back now would equal a type of betrayal. It was a feeling she had not known before, a feeling of wanting to be pulled under and wanting to emerge, a simultaneous plea for intimacy and separation. Who was the plea aimed at? Herself or Clarice?

"God, you'd think the smell of the oil would have gone by now, but it's still very strong," said Ruben

Mona realized that she stank of oil. Her mother looked at her. Did she know? It was always hard to tell with Rosa, but it seemed she knew everything. So during that lunch she decided to assemble a special set of clothes for the shelter—a sort of shelter uniform, she called it to herself.

The next day, Clarice continued. "I had a boyfriend last year. I thought that was love. He said he adored me. Pah! We had sex everywhere. Outside, inside, wherever we could. But then, after some time, he said he didn't want a relationship. He said he wanted to be free to go with other girls. At first, I was upset, like a stupid girl. I didn't know what do with that. But I agreed. I thought, What's the point in trying to convince him? And then, when I went off with another guy and he found out about it, he went mad with jealousy. Nearly killed him."

"Oh wow, really? That must have been confusing."

"Yes." Clarice paused. "After him, I was with this other guy, who thought he was a woman."

"What do you mean, he thought he was a woman?"

"Well, he loved women, he said. But he fucked like a man."

Every time Clarice said the word "fuck" Mona's insides would freeze a bit, but she ignored this feeling for she knew that this was the word she'd have to use too, from now on, if she was to be taken seriously as an equal.

"He wanted to be a woman, he said, he thought women were superior to men, so he would pose for me sometimes as if he were a girl. He'd put his dick between his legs, you know, so it looked like he didn't have a dick, and he'd put my bra on, and we'd sometimes get drunk and role play. I was a guy and he was a girl, he loved that. He'd put tights on, he used to buy loads of tights, and then he'd ask me to rip them off. That was quite fun for me."

"Oh my," Mona said. "I didn't even know such things existed."

Clarice offered her a cigarette and said, "Oh yes, my dear, all kinds of shit exists in this town of ours, under the watchful eye of the President and the parents and the school teachers. And under the watchful eye of this thing," she said, pointing to The Invention. "I swear it's fucking alive, this machine, it's like it's listening to my every word."

Mona looked at The Invention, and indeed, the machine appeared as if it had been billowing under the sheet the moment before, but suddenly stopped, not wanting to be detected.

"Nah, it's just a weird machine that doesn't work," said Mona, mostly to herself.

"Anyway," Clarice continued, "one of my classmates was fucking a philosophy teacher in the toilets after everyone had left school, that happened the other day. Plus everyone smokes in the school toilets. It's a crazy world out there. But I repeat, I don't want to marry anyone. The guys here are stupid, and a woman is imprisoned by marriage."

Mona nodded.

And so Clarice told Mona her stories, and Mona had no idea if they were true, though she did believe them since she had yet to acquire experiences of her own. But the stories flattened her, for her entire concept of the outside world and its structures fell apart with them. The stories gave her a sense of speculation, of wonder when she walked down the street. Who was doing what to whom and how, and why? Clarice was also the first and only person who had asked Mona if she masturbated.

Mona timidly nodded, said, "Sometimes" in a choked voice.

"Just like Lenin said, Learn, Learn, Learn," Clarice insisted, "I say, Masturbate, Masturbate, Masturbate!"

She roared with laughter and Mona pretended to roar, although she was really quite uneasy. All their confessions remained buried inside the fallout shelter. She thought of Diogen saying that fallout shelters were actually tombs, and she thought that, in a way he had not intended, he was right. Mona wanted to confess the greatest thing of all for her—that she thought she preferred girls to boys, and that most of all she preferred Clarice, though it was becoming quite clear that Clarice did not feel the same way.

Chapter 30

RUBEN WAS GETTING ready. He was packing his suitcase. Undergarments: several. Thermal underwear, long johns: yes. He had a list, and he was checking off items. He had prepared all the wardrobe necessities. One copy of the *National Manifesto*, check. He let the book drop onto his folded clothing. Shaving kit, check. He heard the front door close; Diogen had gone out. Ruben was still angry with his brother for spoiling the party, embarrassing the family in front of all the neighbors. Turning up with Nikolai, of all people! The butcher of dogs, infamous for traumatizing his two daughters up in the mountain, where he'd taken them mushroom picking and then shot two poor dogs for barking. He'd said they were rabid! The girls couldn't stop crying for days. Their mother was distracted, came into the shop one day, told him and Rosa about it. Anyway, that's who Diogen was choosing to give his loyalties to, on the day that Ruben had news to deliver, news of such importance. He'd worked his whole life toward this. At least Diogen would be in the army soon, and then, when he came out, he'd be a different person, Ruben knew. Ruben knew everything would be better when Diogen was cured of his lack of discipline, and this mistaken idea of "freedom" he so cherished. Hah! Freedom! He calls that freedom, all that prancing around. Ruben chuckled to himself as he folded his trousers and carefully placed them into the suitcase. He wasn't keen on traveling. He had bought this suitcase for this trip only, since he had no others planned, nor did he wish to make other journeys unless necessary. The only other suitcase he'd ever owned was the one with which he came into town all those many moons ago, and that wasn't any good for *The Blue Dolphin*. That suitcase stank of misery and stone; Ruben kept it in a dark corner of the storage room, but could not bring himself to throw it away. Perhaps he should give it to Robinson to see what miraculous form he could make out of it? A bed for the strays that he'd started collecting outside the apartment building? The old man was really quite crazy, Ruben thought, and the sound of the pigeons was driving him insane, but it was better than that machine. The stench of it! The pigeon shit was not delightful when it wafted in with the southern wind either, but it was better than that monstrous oil. He'd deal with Robinson upon his return, he thought. His gaze fell onto the packed suitcase. What's the point, he had often said, of going anywhere when one's homeland and hometown are so full of wonder? Plus, he didn't like to leave the shop alone, Rosa alone, Mona alone. Diogen alone. Robinson alone. Well, maybe he could leave Robinson alone, he thought. But family, Ruben thought, family is what matters! He suddenly felt like weeping, so full did he become with love for his wife and daughter, now that he was about to leave them for three weeks. He missed them already. His soul felt heavy with fraternal discord. He could not work out what it was between him and Diogen that kept going wrong. It was as if they were two branches of the same tree, growing in opposite directions; one wild and wiry, the other straight and strong.

Rosa came into the room and yanked Ruben out of his reverie by saying, "Two girls, sisters, have gone missing from the village."

"Oh?"

"It was just on the news. Three days ago now, no one knows where they are. Their mother thought they were with their father, father thought they were out. They were our neighbors, I grew up with their mother."

"What, how old are they?"

"Twelve. Twins. God help them. It's started to snow."

She went to the window, tut-tutted at the weather. Outside, snowflakes danced diagonally.

"Do they think somebody kidnapped them?"

"No one knows. Just no trace."

Ruben felt a shiver go through him.

"Mona?"

"She should be home from school soon."

"Okay, make sure she knows I'm leaving tomorrow. I want us to eat together. As for that beast, tell him too, please," he said, pointing with his head toward Diogen's room.

"Robinson? He's on bread and water again."

"No, Diogen."

"He won't speak," said Rosa.

"After doing what he did, now he won't speak? Typical."

Chapter 31

DIOGEN KNOCKED ON Nikolai's window. The snow had settled and Diogen's shoes made a squeaking noise, which he was not happy about—he did not want to attract attention to the fact that he was lurking outside Nikolai's house. Inside the window hung a crooked yellow light bulb, like a decrepit moon. Nikolai peered from behind the curtain, nodded; Diogen heard the lock come undone on the door.

"Come in, brother," said Nikolai.

It was morning. A coffee pot stood on the table. Nikolai put another cup next to his, poured in the thick coffee. His beautiful daughter walked through the kitchen, saying good morning to Diogen, and Diogen nodded to her. He was feeling jumpy.

Nikolai noticed Diogen's nerves and said, "Don't worry, no one knows. It's all wrapped in a blanket." He lowered his voice. "It's a good shotgun, a .30 caliber deer rifle. I've used it a few times. Don't try to get your target from a great distance, it won't do. But anything relatively close, is fine."

Diogen's breathing was shallow. From the day Ivan went back to the army, from the day he disappeared, really, Diogen had entered a state of frenzied fever, some kind of nightmare that was without relief, a kind of countdown to hell, is how it felt. He did not do his exercises, did not go to his hiding spot, did not do much except for sit around or walk around. It had been a week. He could not, did not want to, for the first few days, think of anything else, lest the memory of Ivan and that night together should fade away, but as the days went by, the memory of their night together was starting to disintegrate, furthermore because Diogen had also stopped sleeping, and all he could do was try to keep that memory alive, but the harder he tried, the less he could maintain a grip on any of it. He even had moments when he wasn't sure if it had actually even happened at all. He wrote it all down in a notebook, read it over and over, again and again. He had also written Ivan a letter, which he was planning to hand to him personally. He knew where Ivan was stationed, and he wanted to see him, he wanted to see him desperately. He had tried to contact him by telephone, but the soldier who answered the phone said that Ivan was not allowed to come to the phone.

Diogen finished the coffee and asked for the shotgun. Nikolai handed it to Diogen with both hands, as if he were handing him a newborn child. The stiffness of the rifle sent a shiver down Diogen's spine. He gave Nikolai the cash.

"Thanks, brother. I hope it serves you. I don't want to know what it's for," Nikolai said and laughed heartily. "You should get some sleep, brother, you don't look well."

Diogen nodded. "I've not been sleeping well. A lot on my mind."

He walked out the door. Nikolai's hunting dogs sat out in the yard. They rose as Diogen came out, looked toward him and their noses moved, detecting the smells that wafted out from the house. Diogen went up to them, patted their damp fur. The dogs shivered.

"Don't they get cold out here?"

"They're tough bastards, don't you worry."

It was snowing again. It's like in a fairy tale, Diogen thought, innocent and light, descending from the creamy heavens. He watched a beautiful flake land on the sleeve of his coat, its many strands tiny and perfect. Ah, so much beauty in this cruel world. He put the shotgun in the back of the car, glancing around. The road, and everything around him, was blank with whiteness. Ruben was leaving the next morning, and Diogen did not intend to say goodbye; he was planning to get up before dawn to drive up to the flatlands in the North. To the barracks. To Ivan.

Chapter 32

WHETHER WHAT HAPPENED to Ivan was accidental or on purpose, no one will ever know. But, having spent weeks getting up at 5:00am, washing, saluting the flag, and breakfasting, Ivan was deployed on the cleaning rounds, followed by training. He had received letters regularly, from his mother, from Milena, and from Diogen. He replied to his mother and to Milena; to Diogen he did not. In the afternoons, when the other soldiers were allowed a break after lunch, Ivan and the round-headed soldier were to clean all the weapons. And it was on the day that the round-headed soldier was sick, and Ivan was to clean the weapons alone, that he set off a round of bullets, one hundred and fifty of them, from an M53. He had pressed the trigger, out of curiosity perhaps, or on purpose, for he had fed the bullets into the gun, and the bullets ricocheted against the walls, creating a kind of wasp attack onto Ivan's body, which stood in the center of the room. The bullets danced wildly around him, and many found their resting place in the tenderness of his muscles and soft tissue. Where the flesh was weaker, they went through him; the rest fell onto the floor, surrendering, having found the walls too difficult to penetrate. It all took less than a couple of seconds; the naked eye could not have seen the intricate dance of the bullets. But Ivan, suspended in the last moments of his life, saw the metal pieces, liberated with a spit of fire, propel themselves straight ahead, into the wall, then disperse like a great display of fireworks all over the room, and finally, into his body. Ivan thought this final scene a beautiful one; he felt the prodding fingers of the bullets in his chest, in the soft of his belly, in his legs. Light became darkness and he was forever out of this world.

Chapter 33

RUBEN, ROSA, ROBINSON, and Mona sat at the dining table; there was lamb roast for dinner, Ruben's favorite. The news was on; the search for the missing girls was continuing, to no avail.

"The local police have been searching the area, but so far no trace of the missing sisters has been reported. One can only wonder where they are and how they are coping with these temperatures," said the news reporter.

Ruben turned off the television. "Let's eat, this thing is giving me the creeps."

He looked outside. The clouds had a permanency about them, felt like doom.

"Did you tell my brother that we should eat together?"

"I did," Rosa said. "But he said he had something important to do, that he wouldn't be back until tomorrow."

"That boy is a lost soul," said Robinson, chewing his meat with considerable vigor. "Even those pigeons have more direction than him."

"I thought you were on your Crisis Diet?" said Ruben.

"I gave it up for this special occasion."

"I suppose it's better if we don't say goodbye. We'd just argue," Ruben said before biting into the tender lamb.

"Maybe," said Rosa.

"I'll visit him."

"Hah! Him? The army? He'll last about five minutes in there!" Robinson laughed and banged the table.

Ruben was startled by Robinson hitting the table and a look of worry washed over him.

"Maybe we can send him secret messages via the pigeons," said Robinson, getting lost in that thought for a while.

Rosa wasn't thinking about Ruben leaving, or about Diogen. She was thinking of the missing sisters. Their family lived in the house next to where Rosa grew up; Rosa played with Anka, the girls' mother, when they were little. She had met the girls when they were little. Small, toddling twins with bows in their hair for Sunday church service. The parents had dressed them the same, as was the habit with many twin children of the same sex, so one could never know which was which, and although they had worn different colored stud earrings, to discern them, Rosa always forgot who was wearing red, and who green. This is what she was thinking as she chewed. She thought, I've been to these Civil Protection exercises, I've done all that training. Perhaps I could do something to help. Since hearing about the disappearance, it was all she could think about. Her own daughter seemed so distant these days, Ruben was going away, Diogen was in a world of his own. I can leave food for Mona and Robinson, I won't be away for long. Rosa felt that she might be needed, felt this urge, a pull toward the twin sisters who were God knows where, and it was so cold and snowy out there. She thought of the many ditches around their village, places where it was possible to fall in, the unreliable marshland, the rocks carved with crevasses. Animals sometimes fell in. Why couldn't the girls? Perhaps they were on their way somewhere and fell in and now they were stuck and freezing and starving to death. Rosa's breath grew faster and she forced herself back into the present moment; Ruben's chin covered with grease, Robinson rolling one of his long many-filtered cigarettes, Mona lost in thought.

Mona had hidden her diary. And Rosa had found no more cigarettes. Perhaps it was all a passing phase. She felt that Mona had no need for her at the moment, that the mysteries she had to discover were hers only. There was no space for mother there. One is always so helpless against the forces of life, Rosa mused, thought of her little boy, whom she thought about every day, thought about the girls, and something somehow was connected there, the death of children the cruelest thing of all, of our own death through them, the death we touch when they leave our bodies, and the heart that, from that moment on, is nevermore one's own.

When Ruben left in the early morning, his heart heavy from his brother's absence, Rosa said, "This is something for you to enjoy. Be proud of yourself."

Ruben got on the train. He was to go to the coastal town that served as the navy's headquarters, and from there they would start their journey. Ruben felt his bowels move at the thought of meeting the President. He waved at Rosa, who, he suddenly realized, had not seemed sad to see him go, seemed actually as if she was in a hurry for him to leave, and he waved and the train moved and Rosa waved, and turned and left the station. Ruben sat down and took out the *National Manifesto*; he'd decided to direct his thoughts to something else. Something productive. The first page read: "The Nation can only defend itself against its enemy if it stands united. Like a bunch of twigs, one by one, they can each be broken. Together, they are impossible to destroy."

Chapter 34

"THE FAMILY IS a bourgeoisie concept," said Clarice.

"Eh?"

The lamps were on; the shelter was cold. Clarice was reading a book called *The Origins of the Family, Private Property, and the State.*

"Well, basically, and I totally agree with this, the nuclear family performs ideological functions for capitalism—the family acts as a unit of consumption and teaches passive acceptance of hierarchy. It is also the institution through which the wealthy pass down their private property to their children, thus reproducing class inequality. In that, all women are enslaved—and this is my addition here. Basically, the monogamous nuclear family serves capitalism. Before capitalism, traditional, tribal societies were classless and they practiced a form of 'primitive communism' in which there was no private property—a bit like what the President tried to do here, but in a limited form. I mean, we don't have capitalism, but we still have families, tradition, and all this hierarchy, with the President up there, his wife, and all that, what they're calling the Red Bourgeoisie. It's all about the old norms, repackaged.

Mona nodded. "Yeah, I totally agree."

"Right?" said Clarice. "Like, in tribal societies there were no families as such, but tribal groups existed in a way in which there were no restrictions on sexual relationships. That was really cool. But—and here I quote Engels—'The modern nuclear family functions to promote values that ensure the reproduction and maintenance of capitalism. The family is an ideological apparatus—it socializes people to think in a way that justifies inequality and encourages people to accept the capitalist system as fair, natural, and unchangeable. One way in which this happens is that there is a hierarchy in most families that teaches children to accept there will always be someone in *authority* who they must obey, which then mirrors the hierarchy of boss-worker in paid employment in later life.' Oh my God, that is all so true."

Mona thought about this. She recognized, from what she could see around her, the hierarchy. Diogen was forever flailing, resisting it. Mona had always liked his eccentricity, but lately, she found him embarrassing.

"I think there should be no family, no tradition, no hierarchy. And there should be free love. Everyone should sleep with whomever they please. Forget all this possessive, jealous crap. We're drowning in it."

Mona nodded. "I guess it's true. But I don't know what the world would become if this possessive love was exchanged by a cold love? Isn't it in the end the same kind of thing? Isn't there anything more true than those two options?"

"Let me think about it," Clarice said. "Anyway, I think I want to go and join the student protests up in the capital. They really speak to me, you know, they've been out there for weeks now, protesting about the way socialism has lost its way."

With their hands wrapped around tin cups of hot tea, the girls sat in the freezing shelter. Mona felt happy, despite the cold. Clarice and she convened in the shelter every day, read, wrote, talked. Though it was mainly Clarice talking, about various social issues. Mona listened. She felt she had much to learn from Clarice. She felt that these days were a kind of magical bubble that might burst at any moment, and she did not want to miss out on any of it. Or on any of Clarice's thoughts. And she wanted to give her the letter, declaring her love, felt it was the only honest thing to do, the only courageous thing to do. But she was too cowardly. Still, she tried, one day, to broach the subject.

"Clarice?"

"Hm?"

"What do you think if two women fall in love? Like, what do you think if two women fell in love and they could live together, like, say, two wives," she said, forcing a laugh to hide her embarrassment.

"Oh, I think it's cool," said Clarice. "I just don't think that our society is ready for it, you know, everyone here thinks it's abnormal. But, why not, two women, it would rock. Although I still think these closed relationship forms are all wrong, even between two women, you know."

Mona nodded, said, "Yeah."

They went back to their reading.

Mona's heart beat quickly.

Chapter 35

RUBEN, READING THE *National Manifesto*, was getting drowsy. The sound of the train, clickety-clacking along the tracks was like a memory of his mother's long forgotten beating heart, that came to him at that moment from some primal part of his self, a memory of himself when he, like all the rest of humanity, started out on life's journey inside the warm and soothing carriage of his mother's body, just like now, inside the warm train carriage with the velvety seat that felt so comforting under his cheek. Ruben had a strange recollection of himself as that pink transparent form, attached to the cell of his mother's body by a cord, and he remembered trying to suck his thumb, letting out bubbles here and there, turning over in the amniotic water and all of it warm, warm, warm. Ruben opened his eyes slowly. The beloved country rushed past the windows. He remembered the President's anecdote of the first time he took a train. The President had been a teenager, expecting great things from the great machine, mainly that it was fast and powerful. But upon boarding the train, the boy was disappointed. He said that it was so slow that if he had gotten off and walked alongside it, the train would not have overtaken him. Ruben chuckled to himself and thought, Ah, the President. He closed his eyes again, and the clickety-clack, the pink womb, the President by the side of the train, everything started to melt into one and Ruben fell into a soft, succulent dream.

He was down in the shelter, with Robinson and The Invention. Robinson was wearing his woolly cap and blue boiler suit, and was surprisingly agile on his feet. Ruben was wearing a beautiful lambskin coat and matching hat; he had seen these on the President, he later recalled. He felt luxurious. Robinson was fidgeting around The Invention and explaining things to Ruben in a slow voice, but Ruben had difficulty grasping what language Robinson was speaking. He could not understand every word, and what he did understand made no sense. Robinson's long cigarette seemed even longer now, and Robinson looked at Ruben, from behind bogglingly thick goggles; his eyes appeared miniscule. "I've made more filters, now I'm also using oats and bamboo," he said, suddenly comprehensible, raising his cigarette into the air and putting it into his mouth. He turned away again and stood, motionless for a while, the long cigarette hanging from his lips. Standing like that, Robinson reminded Ruben of a gray heron standing by the side of a pond, motionlessly watching the water. Is a heron expecting to see where the fish are, Ruben thought. Where the flies are? What is Robinson doing?

"I was speaking Esperanto, boy!" Robinson suddenly said.

This was when Ruben decided that he wanted to get out of the shelter, for he found the smell of the oil suffocating and he didn't want his beautiful jacket and hat ruined by the stench, and The Invention and Robinson were quite disturbing, and here he was, in his dream, openly regretting and admitting to himself that he was regretting bringing Robinson into the family home. As if his troubles with Diogen weren't enough!

Ruben wanted to get up and leave the shelter, but he realized, with great horror and surprise, that he had been tied to a chair. With the remainders of the pigeon cage! Had they dismantled it? He could not recall. He said, "Robinson, why have you tied me up?" Robinson said, with a small and perfectly evil laugh, "Because you will now see into the future. You will see all the hell that will unfold." And he started to turn on The Invention. It appeared alive. An evil ally to evil Robinson, Ruben thought. It emitted a great light onto the wall and wagged its metal tail with an abundance of joy. Images started to flood the wall, there was Mona and Rosa and Diogen and Ruben shouted, "No! No!" and shut his eyes and then felt the cold fingers of Robinson upon his face, saying, "Don't worry, I have something that will help you keep your eyes open."

Ruben opened his eyes and shuddered a yawp. His heart was galloping. He was on the train. He was drenched in sweat. It was moments before he could get a grip on reality, the train, the man next to him eating a sausage and smacking his lips. "There is no horror film of the future," Ruben said to himself, "no film, no film at all, it was just a dream." The train had stopped at a station. People were getting on, bringing in the fresh air and different smells. Ruben tried to collect himself and root out the terror from his heart.

Chapter 36

ROSA'S HEART WAS like that of a hunted doe that morning. She could hear its pounding in her head. After Ruben had gone, she went home, changed into her Civil Protection clothes, which included a pair of waterproof olive trousers, under which she put on a pair of thermal tights—keep warm, the instruction booklet for helping civilians had told her—a thermal shirt, a waterproof, windproof jacket, big bulky boots, a hat, and ear warmers. Rosa was fully dressed, and ready in her soul. She left a note for Mona: *There is lunch on the stove for you and Robinson, just warm it up. I won't be back until after dark. Kisses, Rosa.* To Robinson she gave the same message, verbally, but the old man was too engrossed tending to his pigeons; he was tying a small piece of wood to a pigeon's leg. The bird flapped its wings against Robinson's thick grip.

"Samuel has broken his leg again," he said, not looking up. "Poor thing, he never learns."

Rosa went to the garage. No car. No one really ever used the car, and now that she needed it, it wasn't there. Diogen must have taken it. But where had he gone? What a thing. She wondered what to do. Vlatko, the frame maker, opened his door after she rang the neighbor's doorbell.

"Good morning, Vlatko."

"Good morning Rosa, how are you? Why are you dressed like that?"

Rosa said, with a nervous laugh, "Oh, I need to go to the village to help my sister with something outside and these are the only bad weather clothes I have."

There was no sister in the village, but Vlatko didn't know that and she didn't feel like telling him the truth.

"Oh," said Vlatko.

"I need a favor."

"Yes?"

"Diogen's taken the car. I thought he'd be back by now, and I need to go to the village quite urgently. Can I borrow yours?"

"Yes of course, just make sure you pour the antifreeze in at night, it's so cold outside." And he gave her the keys to his Lada.

"Thank you Vlatko, you've really saved me."

She went into the garage and got into the shiny Lada, which was as cold as a grave. Rosa rubbed her hands together, started the fitful engine. She drove out of town. The road was slippery, her pace slow. The town went past her, covered with snow. People's faces crimson with the roughness of the wind.

"The Nation is freezing," said Rosa.

She turned on the news. The signal was creaky. She made out, through the fussing, that there had been no progress in the search for the twin sisters. She had brought all the materials, in case they were found.

"Who knows what the police have, they're normally quite useless," she said out loud to herself.

If Ruben had been there, he'd have told her not to say that about the police, he'd have said that they were doing their best.

But Ruben was not there. Rosa found out, when she reflected slightly, that she was relieved that he was not there. Was she being disloyal? She thought not. He was away, doing what he loved best—serving the President. And Rosa felt that perhaps she could finally do something useful, rather than just run the shop. She had put up the CLOSED sign. Perhaps if Diogen returned soon, he'd reopen. Where was he? Where had he taken the car?

The village of her birth was 15 kilometers out of town. The road was winding, and Rosa drove carefully. Trees were pointing at the gloomy sky, interrupted by pine trees that stood in resolute triangles. The countryside was covered in snow that reached up to the knees; Rosa hoped with all her heart that the poor girls were alive. Magpies made a cricketing, rattling noise, that hacking cough cry of theirs; they sat on the frozen ground together with the crows, pecking with their strong beaks, trying to find dead things in the snow.

Rosa arrived at her old house, a dead place where now no one lived. She looked up at the three pines that were planted when some of her brothers and sisters were born. One had grown to the sky, the other two had remained dwarfish. The tall one had been planted when her sister, Nada, was born. Nada suffered from ill health all her life, and died early. Rosa always thought that perhaps it was the tree sucking up her life energy, but of course, this was irrational. She walked around the house. The walls had fallen in. The house of the family of the missing twins was at the back. Rosa walked through the snow, called out "Heeya!" as was customary. No one responded. She knocked on the door, and soon enough Anka answered.

"Praise be to Jesus."

"And to Mary," answered Rosa.

Anka looked like hell.

"I've come to help search for the girls," said Rosa.

Anka motioned her to come in. She was home alone. Her husband was in the fields, searching, Anka said.

"Sit down."

Rosa sat. Anka brought out coffee and grape brandy. The women drank the brandy first, straight down.

"When my mother died," Anka said, "she cursed me. I had left my first husband. He was beating me. I had bruises the size of summer plums on my face. He'd come home and drink and go straight for me. The twins had to watch it all. So I left him, I left the village. I was married off in the neighboring village."

"I remember," said Rosa.

"I came home, but she wouldn't look at me. Father let me stay, said my husband was a beast. I came back with the girls. It was a disgrace, my mother said. To be a wife who was discharged, that's what she said. Now no one will ever have you. But I went and got a job, and that's where I met Ante. That bastard never gave me a divorce. But then he died. There is a God in Heaven, I tell you, and I married again. It was scandalous in the village, but we thought, when people see that we are decent hardworking people, they'll forget." She paused, scratched the fabric of the tablecloth a little with her fingernail. "But my mother cursed me. She said happiness will never be yours. Those were her parting words from this world, aimed at me. I'd only just remarried. Father had died the year before."

Rosa saw the black and white picture of the old pair. The mother had a slight moustache, the father a large one. They were both serious.

"For years everything was okay. Ante is a good man. We work the land, live off what we make. The twins grew up in a peaceful home. And now this. It's my mother, from somewhere, working that curse."

Rosa said, "Come on Anka, you know that sort of stuff doesn't exist. We'll find them. All sorts of dark thoughts come to one in a time of crisis. We'll find them. Tell me what happened the day they went missing."

Anka said that the girls had gone out, probably to go into the next town, which they sometimes did on foot. It wasn't so cold that day. She thought they were with Ante, pulling up cabbages. When Ante came home and found they were not there, he asked where they were and that's when they realized that they had not returned. They waited and waited, but the girls did not come, not in the morning, not the next evening. Then they called the police.

"But the truth is, the police are doing little. It's the hunters and people from the village who are out searching," Anka said, looking right at Rosa. "I am sure it's your own grief that makes you understand mine."

Rosa had to swallow hard.

"I am grateful for anyone willing to look."

Anka didn't cry, as such. Her eyes were two permanent pools of grief, her head in a scarf. She too was like Mary, watching her crucified son.

Rosa walked across the flat snowy plains that stretched behind the village. There was a distant barking of dogs. The wind was cutting. The snow fell into her eyes and chilled them. Rosa had been deemed "exceptional" as a Partisan. She was known for her incredible dexterity, logical thinking, and endurance. Also her memory. And here she was, in the middle of the field, binoculars on, her back straight. She was a huntress, a Diana. She felt like she understood it all. The deer tracks, they led into the woods; the hooves of a singular boar, covered by snow. She remembered everything from when she was a child; the way they used to go tracking, understood where each animal lived and how it behaved and when it came out in search of food. She remembered everything from the war. There were wolves when she was small; there were wolves in the war. There were wolves now; they came down to get the sheep and the chickens in the night. Jackals, too.

She tried to spot the others, saw several black figures in the distance, walked toward them. The land was flat, and in the summer the fields were busy with mosquitoes, dragonflies, crickets, grasshoppers, frogs. The reeds tall, swaying this way and that. Now everything was white, like the surface of the moon, and Rosa was a lonely explorer, an olive dot on the horizon, moving forth. She administered her fluorescent armband, to be visible from a distance.

When she reached the search party, she saw that they were volunteers from the village, and a couple of policemen who were mostly ill equipped. The villagers, all men, were the hunters. They had rifles, tall boots, and squinting eyes; theirs were the rough faces of men who bore the elements. Several dogs ran around. And Ante, of course. Looking lost, repeating, "Oh dear, they must be so cold, wherever they are," his breath a storm of vapor. They had been looking for three days. Nothing. Rosa found out what areas they'd covered.

"There are some pits over to the north, let's try there," she said.

"The abandoned mines?"

"Yes."

So they went north, and they searched. The day was short, and they searched until nightfall. The snow fell and fell. Their boots creaked. No one talked. Every so often, they yelled "Marina! Ana!" to one side, "Marina! Ana!" to another side, "Marina! Ana!" to the ground, "Marina! Ana!" to the sky. No one answered, save the echo of their voices.

Chapter 37

AFTER ROSA HAD taken the keys to Vlatko's Lada, he panicked. Does she know, he wondered, does her husband know? Jesus God, why did I say yes?

The day before, Boris Pavlovich, the painter, and a group of his friends—whom Vlatko had thought intellectuals and men of certain social standing and socialist thinking, in line with the President's thinking—had come to his workshop, which occupied a large room at the back of Vlatko's apartment, and asked him, no, told him, to hide a stash of shotguns for them. Vlatko had heard rumors about rebel groups starting to form in the country, but he had no idea that Boris or anyone he knew might be involved. Vlatko tried to refuse, but Boris said he knew that Vlatko's stroke had been caused by the stress of owing money to the gambling chief in the Gypsy quarters, where Vlatko had, admittedly, gone for some months and spent all his earnings in his attempts to forget all the failings of his life; he had lost so much money that he and his mother had to sell most of their belongings to return it, and Vlatko had gotten himself into a considerable amount of trouble, and was still chipping away at his debt.

"We'll pay back the rest of your debt. You keep this here and keep your mouth shut. If there is ever a leak, you can be sure you will be served a main course of death, with a starter of torture," said Boris lyrically.

Vlatko felt he had no choice. Plus, clearing the debt was an attractive proposition. The men, with Boris at the lead, came to Vlatko's house daily, occupied the kitchen table and spoke of how they might organize the rebellion. They spoke of being sick of the state of the economy, the single-party system, the way their national symbols were not allowed to be displayed—for why not put an eagle or a cross or a crescent moon just as you might put a star—and they said they wanted power back. They discussed how best to connect with other rebel groups, which, according to Boris and his men, existed all over the Nation.

Vlatko, who was now spending quite a lot of time peering out of the frame of his window rather than framing pictures, had noticed men in parked cars trying to look inconspicuous and he was sure that it was the secret police, staking out his apartment on an anonymous tip about weapons and rebels. Vlatko was sweating with nerves, was hot and prickly all over and scratching himself. Oh dear God if I had only not gambled then I would not have been in debt and then these stupid bastards would not have been able to blackmail me, dear God, what to do now? Vlatko remembered his uncle, who had been a great lover of that old Soviet with a large moustache, as was fashionable at the time, and how he had been arrested for loving him, and love him he did, had a great big photograph of him on his living room wall, and refused to take it down. "They are our brothers!" he'd said every day. "They helped us when we needed it most." Vlatko's uncle ended up arrested and thrown onto that ghastly big island that had not a single tree on it and where everything was bashed either by the deadly sun or the maddening wind, its inhabitants terrorized nonstop. Vlatko shuddered, thinking about his options, either be killed by those stupid bastards or be arrested and thrown into prison, or worse, by the secret police, or maybe he could just move, run away, something, but then they'd find the weapons here and then it would look suspicious. Spiraling into anxiety, Vlatko decided that he'd suffocate and that he should go out for a walk to get a grip on himself, and as he walked he thought he saw that old car move, with the men inside, who he had seen sitting and watching.

Chapter 38

DIOGEN HAD DRIVEN for eight hours. His eyes burned. He looked, and felt, deranged. He arrived in the small town at midnight, and checked into Hotel President. Before he went in, he looked in the trunk, at the rifle. It was safely wrapped in its blanket. The hotel stood in the shape of a beehive, with lozenge amber windows. The focal point of the lobby was a six-foot tall photograph of the President in his famous white uniform. Diogen went upstairs and collapsed without taking his clothes off, a dead man. Before drifting off to sleep, he noted that he stank.

He dreamed of old Fatima saying, "There's a darkness ahead, dear Diogen. Beware of this darkness." Diogen had been so desperate and lost as to what to do, that he'd visited Fatima, in the oldest part of town. Fatima read the future and relieved curses. Everyone knew of her and many went to her in precisely the desperate state that Diogen was in. He knocked on the wooden gate on a cold afternoon and Fatima appeared, a tiny lady with crooked legs that were shaped like an "O." She nodded at him and said, "Come on in, don't worry about the dog." Diogen followed her across the yard, into a shed. The dog, an ancient St. Bernard, sat heavily on the ground, trying to peer through sagging, limp eyelids. Inside, she told him to sit, and without asking any questions, threw a pink blanket onto Diogen's head and said, "*Bismillah rahmani rahimi*," and carried on with the Islamic prayer, while also lifting a pot toward Diogen's head. He watched her through the blanket. She lifted the pot to the head, the heart, and the knees; finally, she took off the blanket, holding the pot in her wiry fingers. "There's a darkness ahead, dear Diogen. Beware of this darkness. Someone you love is descending into darkness." Diogen woke up with a start.

He knew where the barracks was, he had checked the map. He showered, dressed, and shaved. He descended the stairs. The President stood there, watching him with a benign expression as if to say, Upon your own free will, dear Diogen, do what you wish, choose your own actions. Diogen's stomach was heavy. He drove to the barracks, parked, walked across the rail tracks, and entered a small cement shed with REPORT HERE above a round window.

"Good day, comrade," said a soldier with a long nose and a shining red star on his green hat.

"Good day, comrade."

"I have come to visit Comrade Ivan Ivanovich? I believe he is serving in these barracks."

The soldier eyed him up and down.

"Your name?"

"Diogen Maric."

The man said, "Wait here," and walked across the yard.

There were soldiers, walking up and down in their uniforms, lugging things, pushing wheelbarrows. Diogen tried to spot Ivan, but he was not there. He waited. Impatience. He felt the frenzy returning, the chaos of his insides, his intestines, his soul, his heart, his brain, his breath, it was all whirling, just like it had been for days. He looked over at the soldiers, thought of himself among them, immediately felt like he was running out of air. Ivan had told him, "The army is where you learn to tolerate. You sleep on bunk beds. You fight with the man who's below or above you on the bed, and every morning you have to see that fucker's face. So you learn to let stuff go, to make a difference between things. And there are absolutely all kinds of people in the army—urban and rural, educated and illiterate. And they are all with you all the time, and collaborating with everyone is what makes life possible."

The man came back. "Ivanovich cannot receive visitors, except family members. He's been punished. And there's no use waiting, his punishment is three months long."

"Punished? For what?" said Diogen.

Was he not tolerating people? he wondered. Were people not tolerating him? How can anyone not tolerate Ivan?

"That's military matters, not public information."

Diogen exhaled for what felt like forever.

"I drove eight hours straight to see him," he said. "Can't he come out to say hello at least?"

"Comrade I'm sorry, but these are the rules."

"Does he know I'm here?"

"He does."

Diogen walked out and leaned against the window. In his breast pocket he had a letter he had written to his lover, really a mash of pages.

"Can you give him this letter at least?" he asked.

The solder took the envelope. "I can do that."

"Please make sure he gets it. If anything changes, tell him I'm staying at Hotel President."

The soldier nodded and went back to what he had been doing. Diogen walked to the car. On the way back to the hotel, he stopped at a bar. He felt as if his heart was the *Titanic*, and the *Titanic* had just sunk, taking down all those unfortunates with it. His soul was also the *Titanic*. He was the *Titanic*. There was nothing left to live for.

The television was on in the bar. They were running a report about two sisters who had gone missing, near his hometown. "No traces have been found, but the search goes on," the presenter said. Diogen ordered a drink, then another. By the time he left the bar, it was night. In his room, the President's picture hung on the wall. Diogen took it off, spat on it; the spit rolled down the President's cheek. Then he embraced the rectangular frame and wept. He stayed in the hotel the next day. He waited. There was, he thought, a glimmer of hope, maybe, maybe he'll turn up. Run away for a moment, but how can he run away from the army, and especially if he is punished, and what is he punished for, Ivan is so obedient and good, must have been something very bad, oh dear Ivan, and Diogen so wished to hold him in his arms one more time, just one more, though really, he wanted to hold him in his arms forever, here, in Hotel President, or wherever, and he waited and wept and wept and waited. Ivan never turned up.

Ivan had been told that a man called Diogen Maric had left a letter for him, just before he was to clean the firearms. That he had wanted to see him, but that, as Ivan knew, was impossible due to punishment prohibitions.

At the end of the following day, as darkness fell, Diogen got in the car and drove back. When he reached town, at dawn, the familiar lights glittering in the valley, he stopped by the side of the road. He took the rifle out of the boot, loaded it. He thought—I can't go to the army. Ivan won't see me, won't answer my letters. He's to marry. I'll never have another love, I'll never love another. Diogen pulled the trigger. His was a purposeful aim, there was no doubt about it. The gun's fire flashed for a brief moment into the starlit sky; it had stopped snowing, the heavens had cleared. Somewhere, a dog wailed at the moon.

Chapter 39

MONA AND MAIA had been called into the Headmistress's office that morning. The Headmistress wore a mask of thick foundation and red lipstick, which she administered each morning, like an ancient warrior before facing the world. Mona had not ever spoken to her privately before, and at first both she and Maia thought they were in some kind of trouble.

"Has anyone seen you smoke?" said Maia.

"I don't think so," answered Mona. "Why would they be calling you in if that was the case?"

"Oh yeah," said Maia. "I was swinging from the trees behind the school the other day, making really loud monkey noises, and the chemistry teacher saw me and told me off."

"Really?" Mona laughed.

They sat on a bench outside the office, speculating, then fell silent and waited. When the office door opened and they were asked in, the two girls walked through the door with heavy feet, as if going to trial. The Headmistress told them to sit down and started speaking, all the while checking her hairdo in the glass case behind them.

"Girls. You're both exceptional students. Your parents are, as you know, also in service of the President. You've thus been selected by the school to take part in the local dance at this year's Youth Day, which, as you know, is broadcast directly to the President, in the capital. Rehearsals start next week, with the chemistry teacher, Mrs. Grebenc, who as you may not know was once a ballerina."

Maia and Mona looked at each other. Relief! But they had no idea, either that they would be invited to participate in the dance, or that Mrs. Grebenc had been a ballerina. Mrs. Grebenc was tiny and tough and wore an exclusive combination of skirt and blouse suits and kitten heels, no matter the weather. Her nails were claws, painted red or purple, and with them she'd tap on a student's notebook impatiently if the work was unsatisfactory.

The girls were excited to be selected to dance at the Youth Day ceremony. The date of the President's actual birthday was a mystery, like many facts of his private life, but Youth Day was marked as his birthday for the Nation. It was speculated that the President was born some weeks before Youth Day, but he never bothered to clarify, and the government, led by the single political party of which the President was president, had first marked the day at the end of World War II. It was the same day that the President had been very nearly annihilated by the Germans, who mounted an attack upon the location where he happened to be at the time; this was one of the Nation's favorite tales, told to every child. There had been a roaring air raid and a shower of parachuting soldiers, in an attempt to kill the man himself and destroy all the key defense positions. The President was badly wounded. The Nation had pictures to prove it: the President with his shoulder bandaged, but maintaining his serenity and strength. The President Shop had one such photograph framed in a central position, as an inspiring message of personal power and a reminder of the President's sacrifices. So, it was possible that although this day was not the actual day on which the President had been born into this world, it was the day he was born again—by defying death—and the day the Nation had been born, symbolically.

The following year, when the Nation was newborn and rising from the cinders of destruction, Phoenix-like, like the rest of Europe, the youth from the President's village organized a celebration of the President's birthday. They carved a wooden baton containing handwritten birthday notes for the man, and ran the length of the several hundred kilometers from his birth village to the nearby provincial capital, where the President happened to be on the day. They delivered it to him, shook his hand, and the youth exchanged kisses on cheeks with the President. The baton, which by the kilometer had become more and more filled with messages of love and felicitations, was handed from one runner to the next, from one hand to another, and as years went on and the Nation made the celebration official, the baton's route stretched across the country, touching the crucial points that in some way marked the national liberation struggle, so that the youth ran across towns, villages, mountains, valleys, seas, rivers, and lakes (though the larger watery runs were, of course, covered by boat), all culminating in the Nation's capital, where the President awaited. The TV and radio stations gave live broadcasts of the baton's whereabouts. The larger provincial towns would welcome the baton's passing through with their own, smaller-scale synchronized dance performances, in which young people who proved themselves exceptional for any reason would participate. Dressed in the colors of the Nation—blue, white, and red—they would form a spectacle that mirrored the grand finale in the capital, their bodies moving in unison and making the shapes of the five-pointed star, the flag, the hammer and sickle, and sometimes even the President's face.

Before the girls left her office, the Headmistress said, "As the years have gone on, the number of the baton carriers has swelled, from several thousand in the first post-war years, to one-and-a-half million today. The route of the baton this year is 96,000 kilometers. You will witness the baton being passed on, from one hand to the next, and take part in this long line of the physical, human connection of all of the Nation's people. The baton's power becomes greatness by virtue of the number of hands that have touched it along the way. It is a direct link between us, the people, and the President. It is the powerful message of love and union between the people and their leader."

"Oh my god," said Maia when they left the office. "We are going to be the coolest ones in class."

Mona imagined herself dressed in red, blue, or white—for it would be no other colors—in a sea of red flags, forming a fragment in a vast number of other bodies, all working to achieve synchronicity through movement. A single jump, or the raising of arms, combined with everyone else's choreographed movements, would explode in a blossoming image of a star or a flower. She was surprised to find that she felt both exhilarated and claustrophobic at the prospect.

The Headmistress had also told them that there was an annual guest of honor at the Youth Day grand celebration in the Nation's capital, where the handing of the baton to the President took place. The guest of honor was always the same person—a quarryman from the Island of Stone, the same island where the master builders of the Partisan Necropolis came from. He earned his permanent spot at the President's side though a heroic saving of the precious baton from the hands of infiltrators from a neighboring country along the Nation's southern border, who wanted to damage the President's reputation and demoralize the Nation's spirit on this important day.

That year, the baton had been vesseled across a large lake that was home to a vast number of migratory birds—a pale pink splatter of flamingoes resting on bony legs, storks flying across, delivering babies, swifts shooting past like monochrome arrows. None of these birds paid heed to the borders. They flew over the lake or landed upon it as they wished, dipping their feet and their beaks into the water and helping themselves to the fish or the insects. But humanity likes to draw lines across soil, air, and water, and then deploy weapons to guard these lines, with a person attached to the weapon. And so the baton also needed to be guarded at all times when approaching the unfriendly border at the south. The strong young quarry worker was chosen to follow the baton's carrier across the lake, swimming behind the boat. As they got close to the border, the soldiers from the unfriendly neighboring country opened fire on the baton's carrier. The young man and everyone around and behind him were wounded. The young baton carrier, struck by pain, dropped the precious stick, but the young swimmer, alert and strong despite himself being shot in the leg, caught the baton and brought it back to the shore. He thus not only rescued the baton, but also gave the Nation a delicious example of courage. From then on, he had a special seat at the celebration, his sun-baked face radiant as he watched the baton placed, at the end of its long journey, into the President's soft hands.

Chapter 40

MONA RAN IN the snow. The cedar looked magical against the sky, its black branches gently flecked with white. Children were throwing snowballs; Mona was walking back from school and got caught in the crossfire. She felt exhilarated to be outside, her face a peach under the red wool hat. Mona knew that Ruben would be delighted by the news that she had been chosen to participate in the dance that paid tribute to the President's birthday, to be performed in two months. She had not seen Clarice, and felt like she didn't want to go down to the cold shelter that day. The smell of the oil had become overwhelming, and she was getting headaches from it. She couldn't understand how the machine still had so much oil to drip and drool. But then, there was Clarice, coming toward her.

"I was looking for you," she said, taking Mona by the hand and leading her into a corner, out of sight. "Here," she said and pushed the key into Mona's hand. "I won't be needing it anymore. I'm going away."

"What? Where are you going?"

"I met this man last week, I didn't tell you about it. I wasn't sure yet. He's from the capital. He is going back, wants me to come along. He's part of the student protests. Oh, Mona! Life is wondrous!"

"But, what about all the things you said, about marriage, the imprisoned woman, the family as a capitalist tool?"

"He agrees with everything. He's a writer too, and says we can live like artists and we can try to put the Nation back on the right path. He calls it Enlightened Socialism. I can't tell you more now, but his ideas are amazing. Don't tell anyone, please. I know you can keep a secret. I'll write to you."

Clarice kissed Mona on the cheek and Mona watched her run off, the key hot in her palm, the kiss like a butterfly's wings, soft against her cheek. She had questions: What about her parents? What about school? What about me?

Mona climbed the stairs, entered the flat. No one home. There was a note from Rosa about lunch. Robinson was not there. She thought about looking for him, but sat down instead, rested her elbows on the table, her head in her hands, like when she was faced with a complex math problem. A man, the national path, running away, Enlightened Socialism—all of it seemed beyond Mona's realm of possibilities. She suddenly felt small, invisible, as if she had disappeared, as if that period of closeness with Clarice had been a dream, and all she was left with now was herself, a lonely tree in a field by some railway tracks in an irrelevant village, the trains either whizzing past her or stopping briefly and moving on, into lives and realities Mona could never be part of. On the balcony, the pigeons flapped their wings and cooed gently.

Chapter 41

IT CAN'T BE said that Ruben was not enjoying his time on board *The Blue Dolphin*. The ship was a beauty. It had sat in the port like a giant, waiting for them—more of a blue whale, than a dolphin. Inside were enormously long corridors that led into all kinds of rooms. Everything was made of the smoothest oak. There were banquets every day, with mesmerizing food; vegetables were carved into curious shapes: radishes were flowers, carrots were spirals, and beets were five-pointed bloody stars. Ruben was given a cabin with a round window looking onto the open sea. When he was alone in the cabin, he felt like Pinocchio, swallowed by the whale.

"I am a lost little marionette," Ruben said to himself.

They met the President on the first day. He wore dark sunglasses, smiled, and shook each man's hand. The men, in turn, said their name, where they came from.

"Ruben Maric," said Ruben, his hand clammy with nerves. "From the southern region. I run the President Shop and am the keeper of the Golden Statue. I was in the Third Brigade, an artillery man."

"Ah," said the President, "what a pleasure to meet you."

To the next man, from the center of the country, a military officer, the President said, "Ah, what a pleasure to meet you."

Ruben watched the President. He was a great man, Ruben thought. He had not hoped to talk to the President, like a pal might. He had known that this trip was about something else, about instilling a sense of unity. But the President did not seem well. His movements were cumbersome. It had been speculated that he had coronary disease, and that one of his legs had thrombosis, which was evidently the case, since the old man had a cane and a heavy limp. Ruben felt a weight in his heart. The President, this great man, is as fragile as the rest of us, Ruben thought. He knew, of course, that the President had been wounded in the war by a German air strike, and that had it not been for the President's dog, Rex, who threw himself on his master and thus saved his life, the man who built the Nation would not be standing there, on the thick teal carpet of *The Blue Dolphin* reception area. For that matter, the Nation would not be there. At least not in its current guise, Ruben thought. Dear God, who knows what would be here! Ruben, like every other citizen of the Nation, had seen pictures of the President from the war, his shoulder bandaged, but this had just served to show how brave and human, and, of course, how strong the President was, in spite of everything. Ruben knew what war was, and had fought under the President's leadership. And the President had done some excellent things for the Nation, had given them jobs, raised literacy, built roads, all in the name of raising the Nation to be of a top class, a World Standard Nation, and at this Ruben felt his chest swell with pride. But Ruben was looking at an old man, a marvelous old man, but a man who had evidently enjoyed the last two or three decades with rich food, rich clothes, all kinds of luxuries. His hands were manicured, his clothes immaculate; the President was known for his great taste in clothing, even as a young man, and it had long been clear in his choice of suits and uniforms that he liked to dress well. But it was a far cry from the image of the young soldier that Ruben so admired. The President also had an exclusive island upon which many exotic animals had been placed for his enjoyment, among them zebras and giraffes, gifts from faraway allies of the Nation. They were to visit that island on this trip. Ruben was keen to see the private pleasures that made up the President's life now, but he also felt uneasy, he realized as he stood aboard the luxury yacht, about witnessing things that were a world away from the idea of the struggle that was at the heart of the Nation, the struggle against Evil, the struggle for Good, the struggle for Unity, the struggle for Brotherhood, against Fascism, all those values that Ruben was willing to fight for and give his life for, then and now. Where was the struggle in an exotic private island where you could watch an elephant graze in the midst of the Mediterranean? Although, he quickly reminded himself that there were theories of elephants being native to Europe many centuries ago, possibly millennia, Ruben couldn't remember now, so perhaps there was a context to it, Ruben thought, perhaps it's possible to ignore this and see it as an attempt to repopulate the continent with animals that had been made extinct?

After the meeting and greeting, there was a speech by the President. There was danger in the country, of rebellion. They needed to look out for it. The students were protesting, the nationalists were protesting, all the things that they had fought to eliminate—such as the differences between the Nation's peoples—were surfacing again. And this was a great danger, the President said: "Brotherhood and Unity cannot fail—we must care for it as we care for the apple of our eyes, for if it fails us, we are headed down a long, painful, bloody path."

The audience clapped and nodded. Ruben remembered his dream of Robinson, and a great wave of anxiety coursed through him. *The Blue Dolphin* sailed. It was a cloudy day. It had not snowed in the port town, but the wind was up. The ship moaned and danced on the waves. In the afternoon there was free time, to be followed by dinner and speeches. Ruben went to his cabin to rest. He felt uneasy. Some of the other men—there were a total of twenty-five guests—stayed upstairs to have a drink and smoke and talk. Ruben felt unsociable, could not understand what was going on with him. He lay down on the small bed. He looked out of the window at the foamy waves. The sea was like a silken gray cloth, being pulled up here and there by invisible threads. He felt a terrible longing for home, for Rosa, for Mona, for Diogen. He felt a terrible guilt about calling the commander about his brother. Now that he was far away, none of it seemed important, it did not matter, he thought, that Diogen should be straightened out like a piece of crumpled cloth. He remembered the little gasping baby upon his chest, Diogen's little body, so fragile, his grip strong. He remembered the toddling boy, who would curl up to him at night as he slept. The dancing boy, who found so much joy in song.

Ruben wept.

Chapter 42

DIOGEN HAD SHOT at himself, but not being a rifle expert, the bullet ricocheted and he somehow managed to shoot off three toes on his right foot. He fainted with pain and bled. A pair of shepherds discovered him by the side of the road, just before dawn. The men, upon seeing him there with the rifle at his side and a discarded picture of the President, which Diogen had taken from the hotel room, panicked and ran off to find a telephone and call an ambulance. They crossed themselves all the way.

Next to Diogen was a note that read: *Don't hate me. I just can't do it. Life has no meaning. I tried my best.*

The note was blown off by a gust of wind. No one ever read it. The ambulance came with the whir of lights and noise, and Diogen was transferred into the vehicle where he was connected to all kinds of tubes. The medics concluded that he would live, and it would be somewhat complicated to walk at first. The nurses tried to call the house to inform the family, but no one was home.

All the while Diogen was unconscious, dreaming. He dreamed that he and Ivan sat by a river that was like the one they both so loved, but not that one, and that Ivan was surrounded by dragonflies, which flew around him and landed on his hair. Then those same dragonflies landed on Diogen's hair. They had the most delicious picnic laid out between them, and they smiled at each other and looked into each other's eyes. Diogen was as happy as he would ever be. They looked at the river, where fish jumped out of the sparkling water. The air smelled of orange blossom. Diogen was, he was convinced, dead, and had gone to heaven. When he woke up in the hospital room, alone, or rather with three snoring men around him, he was not sure whether he had descended into hell. He had intended to end his life. But life had not finished with him.

"Oh, you're awake," said a nurse with yellow hair. She was checking the drip that was going into Diogen's arm. "Were you cleaning the rifle or what?"

Diogen looked at her. Said nothing.

"Well, you're alive. We tried to call your house, but can't get hold of anyone. You just rest for now," she said and left the room.

Diogen closed his eyes and saw strange landscapes, the prairie, the savannah, arid alpine mountains. Places he had never seen before. He also saw his older brother, aboard *The Blue Dolphin*, weeping inside a small round window, sitting on a bed like a child.

Chapter 43

THE NURSES BROUGHT Diogen bad tea and called him "darling"; they seemed to like him. Lunch was potato mash and a chunk of meat. Diogen chewed listlessly. His foot hurt like hell. He felt humiliated by this pathetic injury; yet, he was relieved by the thought that at least he would not go to the army. Surely this would do it.

A nurse came in, turned on the TV, and announced, "They've found those two girls."

The TV was suspended in a high corner of the room, so that each patient could see it. But it was so high up that it was hard to make out the picture. Diogen was part squinting, part indifferent. His own sorrows seemed larger to him than anything the TV might report. The screen showed images of two emaciated bodies being carried into an ambulance, covered with the special blankets provided by the Civil Protection unit—there was no mistaking them, they had CIVIL PROTECTION printed in large letters diagonally across.

"Stuck in a ten meter-deep pit of the abandoned mine, some five kilometers from home, these two young women were practically buried alive for seven days and eight nights. It is a miracle they survived. They went out of the house wearing only denim jackets, jeans, and boots, and the sub-zero temperatures, snow, and snow storms mean that for these two girls, hypothermia is guaranteed."

The presenter stood in a snowy field. The trees behind him were charcoal shadows.

"They had been calling for help for days, but it was Rosa Maric, a brave volunteer, who comes from the same village, who finally found them and descended into the pit to save the Anastasijevic twins. What a brave woman indeed. No wonder she is also our National Hero, a Partisan, who had fought in the great National Liberation Struggle as a young woman."

Rosa appeared on the small screen, her eyes straining, her lips twitching a little as she watched the ambulance workers load the girls onto stretchers. Diogen sat up in bed, nearly choked on his lunch.

Chapter 44

AFTER TWO DAYS of searching to no avail, the situation seemed hopeless. The girls had been missing a week already; no one could survive such conditions. The search group had been reduced to the old hunter Josip, and his two nephews, Oto and Efi, who were eighteen, over six feet tall, and rather chatty. The rest had lost hope, had homes to return to, their own worries to tend to. Oto and Efi had been sent by their father to help the search, as an aid to Josip, and "to learn something" their father had said. Oto and Efi were strong and could walk for a long time in the snow, but they lacked any real intelligence, Rosa thought. More of a hindrance, than help. They found the idea of Rosa, or rather, a woman, searching, a woman being able to withstand the physical strain of the cold and walking, they found that very funny and surreal, and mocked Rosa when they thought that she wasn't paying attention. What they did not realize was that Rosa, set in search mode, her senses completely attuned to the world around her, heard all, saw all. It was as if an inner compass was guiding her, as if she were a wild animal, sniffing the ground, noticing every movement in the forest, a rushing of leaves, a movement of a bush.

She watched above for birds, for a murder of crows moving across the sky; if the girls were dead, the scavengers would go for them. She smelled the air. Noticed how it moved behind trees like a whisper. Oto and Efi made faces impersonating Rosa, silly noises that were meant to sound like her.

Tired of these two enormous idiots Rosa said, "I'm going to head east, toward the mines one more time, there is one that we didn't get to the other day. I'll check there. If either of us finds something, fire the light bullets, okay?"

Rosa headed toward the old mine, along the straight path that they had been down a couple days before, and walked past the first lot of coal pits, started and abandoned several years ago. Not enough coal. She walked on, to the one that sat four kilometers further from the rest. It was a dead part of the landscape. No one came here. The woods were where life went on, where mushrooms popped up, where berry bushes prickled, trees blossomed, and pines dropped their cones to the ground. Where, if one was as quiet as a shadow, one could watch a doe lick its baby with divine tenderness. But here, there was nothing. Flatlands. Miners were brought in with their families, housed in the small town nearby. They were transported at the earliest of dawns to work, but hardly anything came out of those pits. So they moved the miners to better underground areas. The ground was porous and over the years some of the mines had collapsed in places and were now open pits. And then, it happened. Rosa heard them. "Help," shouted the little voices. "Help!" For a moment, Rosa thought she was hallucinating. But then she knew what she was hearing. She ran toward the cries.

For years to come, Rosa dreamed of the moment she saw the girls. They were curled on the ground, skeletal. Their eyes were open and their mouths were open, shouting for help, teeth chattering, going in and out of consciousness.

"Oh my god," Rosa said, her breath nearly giving in on her, but she collected herself. "Don't worry, help is here, we'll get you out."

She fired three bullets into the sky. She then tied a rope to a boulder and descended into the pit. Her backpack contained everything she needed to administer first aid. Rosa wrapped up each girl in special Civil Protection blankets, with careful and decisive movements. Then, with adrenaline pumping, making her feel like a young Partisan again working a dangerous secret mission, she put the first girl over her shoulder, told her to hold on, climbed up the rope, laid her on the ground, and wrapped her in another blanket. Climbed down again, put the second girl over her shoulder, climbed up the rope. She saw Josip approach. He had some type of radio and called for help.

The girls looked at Rosa with wonder in their eyes and said, "Thank you, thank you, God from the heavens sent you, thank you."

Rosa gave them warm tea from a flask, kept them wrapped up in many blankets until the ambulance came.

Everyone thought that the survival of the sisters was a miracle. The Nation followed the story, and much of the Nation donated money to the family. The girls were transferred to the capital on a helicopter sent over by the President himself, who had watched the whole thing from *The Blue Dolphin*, alongside Ruben who, upon seeing Rosa, whom he was missing terribly every day, leapt from his chair and shouted, "Rosa? Rosa! Dear people, that is my wife!"

The President said, "Is that not Comrade Rosa? Ah, she was a fine Partisan, one of the best messengers we had. I invited her into the government when the war was over, but she refused, said she did not want to be in politics."

The President chuckled and then added, “She did give a great speech at the State Antifascist Council for the National Liberation of the country, back in 1943, in favor of the women’s vote. It was what won everyone over. Ah, Comrade Rosa, she would have a made a great member of the government. Look at her. Such determination.”

Ruben looked at him and said, “Really?”

She had never told him. He suddenly felt angry with Rosa for keeping this from him—he would have been so proud!

Rosa was awarded a medal for exceptional courage, which she accepted. The girls lost their legs to gangrene. There were newspaper pictures of them in wheelchairs, knitting, looking casual.

When interviewed, one of the sisters, speaking for the both of them, said, “We believe in fortune, and sometimes fortune does not favor you, like when we fell into the pit. Sometimes you’re luckier than anyone on Earth, such as when people like Rosa Maric come to your rescue. The wheel of fortune turns and turns. And one never knows where it will stop. You just have to accept what happens with grace.”

Chapter 45

WHEN CLARICE LEFT, she left a letter for her parents in which she declared that she had gone to "improve the path of Socialism." Her father was enraged and her mother embarrassed, yet she somehow admired her daughter.

Maia said, "I knew she was going to pull something like this."

Mona did not know whether her having known about the fact that Clarice was running off was incriminating, but she decided to keep quiet. There was no way she would have hampered Clarice's plans, even though it might have meant that Clarice would have stayed nearby, if the parents had managed to keep her at home, which Mona doubted.

Clarice had written to Mona once and told her about the student protests, the art and films that were being produced, and all the new interesting people she had met: *Things with that guy didn't work out, I won't go into it, but I'm staying anyway, it's so great to be here and I really feel that the reforms we are supporting will make a difference to our future as a country. I may try to go into the movies, there is so much amazing stuff being made, stuff we back home have never even heard of.*

After a while, Clarice's parents located her, but she refused to return.

Mona wrote a postcard back to Clarice, on which she simply wrote: *Miss you in the shelter. Kiss.* She thought this was enough for now; she never went to the shelter anymore anyway, The Invention's oil had made it unbearable and the place made no sense without Clarice in it. She kept Clarice's letter in her coat pocket, to read whenever she could. It made her feel that Clarice was somehow still part of her life. In the meantime, Mona and Maia practiced for the dance every day.

Mrs. Grebenc shouted out: "And lift!"; "To the left! Come on, show some grace, you look like pieces of dead wood"; "Up! Down!"; "Lift your chins up it's not a funeral!"; "The President will be watching!"

Chapter 46

ROBINSON WAS WORKING on producing a battery that would charge The Invention without using the building's electricity supply. His prototype had to sit in the sun every day, so he camouflaged it as part of the pigeon coop and kept it on the balcony. The time Rosa was gone, and Diogen was gone, and Ruben was gone served him well to do as he wished in the flat for a couple of days, and Mona did not seem to care much about what he was doing; she seemed preoccupied with her own things, girly things probably, thought Robinson. He even put up around town some more notices advertising his museum, and two young people turned up, paid the entry fee even, but when they descended the stairs into the shelter and saw the machine and smelled the oil they said something incomprehensible and quickly left. Robinson did not understand why. He was about to offer them some plum brandy and homemade cheese and really welcome them in the traditional way, but they had not given him the chance. Anyway, he'd taken some money, which he could use to buy several more parts for his next invention—The Truth Detector, which was not the same as a lie detector, but was a more metaphysical kind of concept, one he had yet to work out completely, but which would ultimately help him locate the truth, wherever it was hiding. There was much too much ambiguity in the world, even plants were sometimes healing and other times poisonous, Robinson felt, and one could get lost in the world, especially among humans, and he thought particularly Ruben and Diogen could do with The Truth Detector, since they were often so confused, as far as Robinson could tell, and it was Rosa who understood something, he thought; she was a woman who was like an arrow, but a gentle, kind arrow, if that made any sense, thought Robinson, and he admired Diogen for shooting off his toes, patted him on the shoulder when he came back home, hobbling.

"I'd underestimated you, boy," he said. "But you've done well there, look at all that determination not to go and serve the army!"

Diogen scowled and said, "It was an accident."

Anyway, Robinson thought, just a little longer and The Invention will be ready, I can finally turn it on, my beautiful baby, and he walked around the machine and caressed it, and the machine seemed to enjoy Robinson's attention, it seemed to want to work, to obey its master.

Chapter 47

JUST BEFORE HIS eighty-eighth birthday, the President died. Ruben had returned from *The Blue Dolphin*, fragile and afraid. He cleaned the golden bust with a sense of sadness and had stopped displaying it in the shop. In fact, the shop carried on its work, and saw an enormous boost in trade following the days after the President's death. But Ruben was full of fear. He had seen the decaying state of the President's body, the way he had stalled in his speech, his trembling hands. He had guessed it was coming.

The President's passing opened up a void inside the Nation that was greater than the Bermuda Triangle. The Nation wept for days. The country ground to a halt. There was talk of an assassination, masked as a natural death. There was talk of unrest. There was talk of weapon stockpiling by civilians, of money pouring in from abroad to fund rebellion. Vlatko, from downstairs, had been arrested by the secret police. Weapons had been found in his flat. It was inexplicable that Vlatko was involved in anything of the sort, but there you go, Ruben thought, one never knows. Ruben was worried. No one knew who the next president would be, and if there would again be the President of sorts, or just a president. Who could take over from the President, Ruben thought? It was impossible, the gap left behind him was too large to be filled by anyone. The student protests were over, the secret police had cracked down on everyone they thought had anything to do with the unrest. Ruben met with some of the old Partisans, and they too were despairing.

Diogen, following his accident, had not gone to the army, and Ruben was secretly relieved. They sat together in the mornings, drinking coffee and reading the papers, careful of conversation.

Diogen saw Nikolai when taking a walk. He found walking on crutches difficult, and he had no energy from his heart, for his heart was shattered. Yet, somehow, the physical pain kept him grounded to his body, made his mind steadier. Nikolai drove past him and offered Diogen a lift home.

"Before I take you home, brother, I have to go to the Gypsy quarter," Nikolai said.

"Okay," Diogen said.

The Gypsy quarter, on the outskirts of town, was an encampment of cardboard and tin houses, or boarded up shacks. There was activity everywhere, barefoot children running around playing with a ball or chasing a wheel and hitting it with sticks. Diogen watched them, and when the car stopped, some of the kids came up to his window, put out their muddy palms and said, "Give us a coin," and Diogen gave them a coin. Nikolai told Diogen to wait and got out and spoke to some large men who appeared out of another car, similar to Nikolai's, a beaten up Caddy. No one paid attention to them. The children went back to their game and Diogen got out to stretch his legs. He leaned against the car and looked up at the sky; a flock of seagulls glided across the blue heavens, the birds resting their wings on the air. Some flew away from the huge cloud of the other birds, a diagonal, effortless roam. How magnificent this lightness, this simple moment, thought Diogen, there is no struggle, no effort at all. Why all this suffering, all this struggle? He felt as if, at that moment, he understood Jesus's bleeding heart, the core of love; he felt like embracing all of humanity in its relentless struggle against—or was it for?—love. He looked over at Nikolai and the men; they were standing around the trunk of the men's car, rummaging around. Nikolai walked back with a large, long bag that was, Diogen understood, stuffed with shotguns.

"What's all this?" said Diogen.

They got in the car. Nikolai lit a stinking cigarette, rolled down the window, and blew the smoke out. "There's a growing interest in weapons these days."

Diogen nodded. "So I hear. I managed to get out of the military, but it seems nowadays the military is everywhere."

"Yup," said Nikolai, driving back through the quarter. A large cow sat by the road, chewing cud. Nikolai honked, to startle it, but the cow was unperturbed. "It's easier to do business here, brother, all sorts of shit goes on and the Gypsies don't report anything. The police are not their friends."

They drove on and Diogen wondered what had become of Lament. Everything that happened before the shooting seemed to belong to another world. He cherished the memory of Ivan, held that love in his heart; but the rage was gone. He was broken by his lover's death; some said it was suicide, his mother said it was an accident. Diogen prayed for Ivan's soul every night before sleep, a prayer he had invented himself. He still sang, but his voice was quieter. Apart from his prescribed daily walk, to the river and back, where he watched the cherry trees throw their pink flowers to the ground, he stayed at home. He helped Mona practice her moves for the dance. Occasionally he went to the river in the evening, to listen to the song of the nightingales. They rested on the riverside branches for exactly a month at this time of the year and produced the sweetest sounds known to mankind.

Chapter 48

ONCE THE PRESIDENT was no more, there was some confusion about whether it would be appropriate to deliver the baton, or perform the dance. For whom? Who would be there, in that sacred spot that had been held by the President's glorious presence for decades, to receive their offering, watch them dance? Who would deliver the speech, thought up on the spot, always so moving and beautiful? Would the youth, who were doing all the dancing and delivering, feel that same pride and joy when shaking another's hand? The hand of some mere party bureaucrat? Would their hearts leap? Would they be able to tell their friends with pride and excitement "I shook his hand!" like they used to?

Ruben thought long and hard about this and wondered whether a new leader and the idea of the Nation and its ideals could transcend the absence of the great man and keep the country stable. He could not imagine it himself, but perhaps the youth were more flexible, the idea powerful enough to carry on? He did not know. No one knew.

He asked Rosa about it, and she said, "I doubt it, but perhaps, perhaps, let's see. Our people, like all people, are but sheep in a field, they always need a shepherd—Jesus was a shepherd, wasn't he? Now it just depends on what kind of shepherd we have the fortune to get."

Ruben was surprised by Rosa's answer. He wanted to hear something more soothing. Diogen merely lifted his eyebrow. He was no longer expressing opinions.

After some deliberation, the government decided that things should go on as planned, and came up with a new slogan for the spectacle: "The President Lives On In Our Hearts." It had been decided that the baton would be received by the inheriting president of the political party, symbolically, and so the rehearsals for the dance carried on. Some saw this as pointless now that the President was no longer alive—since the baton was a birthday present for the President, after all—while others thought it was a poignant way to remember him. Others were of the opinion that it was crucial to carry on with and reinforce the President's message of remaining firmly on the Nation's path of Brotherhood and Unity. For the first time, Diogen found himself wishing that the Nation would remember the President's words, especially as he watched Boris going in and out of Vlatko's flat with bags that were reminiscent of Nikolai's. Vlatko had been arrested, but Boris seemed to keep on with his activities.

Ruben was growing listless; there were bags of sadness under his eyes. Rosa worked hard. Mona practiced every day; it was a good way, she found, not to think too much. About Clarice, about her body, about girls and boys—about any of it. She, and the rest of the dancers, were not bothered by who would watch, and why; they were too busy trying to make the dance ready in time. The choreography, a lift, both arms pointing upward, holding a medium-sized hoop, a jump, some kicks, it had to be perfect, all in time with the music. Diogen helped her and either said, "No, no, it's all wrong, do it again," or, "Perfect, perfect, Mona." Even Mrs. Grebenc seemed pleased.

The news showed unrest in the north of the country; people unhappy with their rights, lifting their national symbols into the sky, together with their outstretched arms and clenched fists. They belted slogans into the air. Then they were mostly imprisoned and things seemed to settle down.

All this time, The Invention's battery was soaking up the sun on the balcony, with Robinson's careful, daily assistance. Since Mona had stopped going to the shelter, he had the place to himself, not that their hours had ever clashed, and he had arranged things the way he liked them: a nice armchair, covered with sheepskin; Mona's teapot; his many filters were laid out on the table neatly. And every time he oiled the machine, he rubbed his hands with joy and patted it lovingly, said sweet words to it, such as "You and I are going to make a lot of money, my dear, everyone wants to know what the future brings, and you're going to tell them about it, aren't you?" And the machine would appear to move its projection lens up to get closer to the caresses, purring like a kitten, and Robinson would say, "That's my pet, yes, yes."

Chapter 49

MONA STOOD BEFORE her bedroom window. It was the night before the performance, and she looked out into the darkness. Her reflection was suspended between herself and the world. It was the time of the day when one is able to see the window, the world outside, and oneself in the reflection, and all three images were part of the moment, none more real or false than the other. It's partly how Mona felt about life, so far—that it was a matter of the self reflected in the world and the world reflected in the self, and often she could not discern what was imposed upon what and if any of it made any difference at all. Since Clarice had gone, Mona had dedicated herself to the dance, spring was readying itself for summer. Diogen was home a lot, and he made her listen to the opera; she enjoyed it, she loved Puccini and Mozart, though she tried to stop Diogen singing over it, but she liked it, and with the music she tried to exorcise the sadness of Clarice not being there, of that possibility of love gone. There was no one remotely close to how interesting she had been, the others at school were boring, she thought, there'd never be anyone like Clarice again, that was sure, and so she tried to keep her mind on other things, like the dance, and she was trying to compose a letter to Clarice that would reveal her feelings and be literary and poetic, and deep, and it was taking forever and Mona decided that she'd finish it when she was ready.

She was wearing a red leotard and a shiny white skirt for tomorrow's dance. On her feet she had plimsolls, white and light; all the participating dancers had them. They had signed each others' shoes, to mark their friendship as a group, but Mrs. Grebenc saw it and told them off, so they had to get new clean white shoes for the performance. She felt ready. She felt calm. In the morning, she walked out of her room; Diogen was already waiting for her. Her mother gave her a packed lunch and a Tetra Pak of apple juice, and she walked down the stairs.

Ruben, wearing a pin in the shape of the President's signature on his jacket collar, said, "See you there."

The town stadium was decorated with blue, white, and red, stars and banners, as well as several pictures of the President. National songs blasted out of the speakers, promising to not stray off the President's path, telling the President he was the Nation's flowering rose. Rosa, Ruben, and Diogen had seats in the front area. Robinson had said he was too frail to come; he remained on the sofa in a supine state, letting out small sighs. When Rosa had offered to stay with him he quickly responded, "No, no, no, please go, this is too important for you to miss. I'm just an old ass, who cares if I die?" and laughed. So they left Robinson there. He, of course, had been waiting for the battery to be charged, and today was the day it was ready. He waited for them to leave and picked up the big black box and rushed down the stairs into the shelter.

Ruben wept quietly in his seat. It was awful to know the President was not there, not anywhere in the world except as a decomposing body in the ground. Rosa took Ruben's hand.

Seeing the President's picture and the symbols of the Nation, Ruben felt as if it was all a big joke, it had all been a big joke, and wondered how long they could keep it up.

"What will become of us Rosa, dear?"

"It'll all be okay, don't worry."

Some weeks earlier, there had been a national scandal over the controversial design of that year's Youth Day poster. The poster was always produced by those who won the national competition, and this year it was a group of young designers from the very region that had started the protests. They produced a picture of a young muscular man holding the five-pointed star in his right hand. However, the design was almost identical to the one used in Germany, back in the 1940s, to promote the National Socialist Party. There was an uproar. Ruben was incensed, as were most people. All this, and so soon after the President's death. The Nation saw it as a direct provocation against everything it stood for. But there were those who agreed with the poster's symbolism. "It's a tyrannical state," some said. "It needs to come to an end." The posters were changed. The new poster, with five harmless red stars in a circle, hung among the rest of the decorations at the stadium.

The music started. The dancers came out in a long single-file, light of step. Diogen saw Mona. A white skirt, a red leotard, her auburn hair pulled back, her body lean and quick. Diogen and Rosa and Ruben all sighed. Rosa smiled and Ruben, upon seeing Mona, burst out into a fresh round of tears. Diogen put his arm around Ruben's shoulder. The three watched the Youth of the Nation form shapes with their bodies, perfectly timed to the rhythm of each other and the music; they lifted and moved and created beautiful waves of color, the red, blue, white of the flag, ran around each other and produced a red star, which to Diogen appeared like a starfish, a living organism, made out of the young unified bodies, and it spoke to the sky, sent some secret signals to it. A long column of young men came out carrying dozens of red flags, the fabric licking the air like a long fiery tongue, and they separated and white-clad dancers appeared in the parted red river, and they made formations that resulted in WE LOVE YOU PRESIDENT, spelled out in large white letters made out of human bodies. There was a great round of applause.

Rosa, Ruben, and Diogen sat, mesmerized, watching the performance, the swirling colors, the changing formations that evoked tightly sewed up sequins pushed this way and that to reveal hidden shapes and patterns. Diogen saw the emptiness of the adoration of symbols, but he was moved by this optimism for the first time, perhaps because he sensed that it was too easy to replace the optimism with a great nothingness. Perhaps, he thought, this love and idea of unity, even though it's odd for me, perhaps it's the only way. Look at how nice it is that all these young people have come to dance together, he thought, and surprised himself with the sentimentality that he suddenly felt for the spectacle. Rosa watched and admired the organization, loved the firm bodies, their energy, their vitality. Ruben felt as if a plug had been pulled out at the center of his being, yet he was proud of his daughter. To him, the spectacle seemed empty, strange, devoid of meaning. At the end a young woman, a local sports champion, delivered a speech that promised that the Nation's Youth would carry on the President's message. There was another roaring applause.

After meeting with other families and congratulating each other on the children's performances, the family went for lunch at the National Restaurant where the terrace was shaded by linden and almond trees. The almond blossoms perfumed everything. Spring was at its late afternoon best; the dappled light, the sweet fragrances, the warm air. They ate well: river carp and greens and, for dessert, a wobbly sour cherry gelatin treat. There was wine and beer and for Mona, rose water juice. The company was good. They spoke of this and that, things not related to the spectacle, to the President. Mona wondered if she should quit smoking and wished Clarice had seen her dance. Diogen sang a song. He remembered Ivan's soft hands. Ruben, Rosa, and Mona all listened and clapped. The air was as gentle as a newborn's skin, and there was a sense of a new energy being pulled up from the earth.

Rosa said, "Spring is the hardest season. Earth and all the creatures upon it require a great deal of energy for the rebirth, the renewal, to work upward from the scarce winter resources."

It was not often that Rosa spoke like this, so there was a hush as she delivered her words.

"The secret is to preserve energy, to organize resources wisely, to use autumn's storages patiently over the winter period. It's why bears hibernate. They, like us, are too tied to their locations and too heavy to move to warmer climes with the seasons. Only birds can do that, with their beautifully ordered flocks, collaboration, shared resources, and determination. They use each other's air current to rest their wings, mid-flight, and each bird gets a go at resting and working for the flock."

Ruben felt like crying again. He loved Rosa so. He loved his whole family. The day sparkled with the afternoon sun.

"We must learn from birds. We must always work together," Rosa concluded, "and cultivate love and friendship to make life as beautiful as possible. Without this, all of life's hardships are impossible to bear."

Mona breathed in the fragrance of the air, looked up at the clear sky.

Chapter 50

ROBINSON UNCOVERED THE Invention, patted it, and connected the machine to the black battery box. It made an instant, whirring sound, and Robinson let out a small yelp of joy. He pushed the key into the little hole at the back, just like he had done on the day he was going to demonstrate the machine's wonders to Mona, and a great spot of light showered the shelter wall. A small puff of smoke came out of the machine. Robinson took the little winding handle and yanked it until the machine started to wheeze, and images started to project onto the wall. There was the universe first, the galaxies, wondrous colors and gasses and what Robinson thought was the Milky Way, then the Earth could be seen through the collection of the stars and planets, and Robinson watched all this and thought, Have I really created this machine? My God! He patted The Invention again. The machine gave a little wheeze in response, and they traveled through the cosmos together, Robinson feeling as if he too was being transported on the wings of the machine and the future was his to be seen, and as they neared the Earth, carried through space in all its beauty, there were the oceans, the forests, the birds in the sky. Robinson had no idea where the flight would take him, he felt like Aladdin on the magic carpet. He thought, All my life I have worked toward this, ah how beautiful it all is, and the picture drew closer to Europe and to the seas, and toward their little country, Robinson's and Ruben's and Rosa's and Diogen's and Mona's homeland, and as it neared, Robinson saw they were getting closer to their region, then to their hometown, the very one he was sitting in at that moment, and then he thought there was something wrong with the picture, for there were ruins where the buildings once stood, ruins like burnt out holes in a piece of wood, and there were people in the street running away, and guns shooting and shells falling, and the camera was now amongst the people and Robinson could see Ruben and Rosa and Diogen and Mona, and they were a little older than they were now, and they were running for dear life, and Robinson stood up and said to the machine, "What is this, what are you showing me you silly thing, what's all this nonsense I'm seeing?" But the machine being a machine could not speak and did not care for Robinson's distress, and the picture carried on moving through the familiar streets, and where there had been beautiful things now there was nothing but destruction, and the river was flowing as before, only now it was full of fallen trees and human bodies were caught on the blackened branches, and Robinson stood, wordless, and the picture moved around and out of the town and into the neighboring towns and over the whole land and showed unspeakable things, people in great lines trying to flee, grandmothers desperate, children desperate, mothers desperate, men fighting and starving men behind barbed wire, and Robinson sat down, his knees weak now but unable to peel his eyes off what he was seeing, and he said to himself, "It's a mistake, surely it's a mistake, no one can see the future, this is not real." And as the picture moved onto a military general giving orders to bulldoze thousands of dead bodies down into the ground, Robinson failed to observe that the machine was emitting great amounts of smoke into the room, and as he watched people at a vegetable market murdered by a falling shell, he did not understand that the room was now entirely shrouded in smoke and The Invention was on fire. Robinson watched and wept and did not stand up to put out the fire, he could not move, and the picture kept going on, into this future that was presenting itself through the smoke. Robinson said, "It's the greatest nightmare anyone could conceive of," and the land moved away again and the picture was of a burnt down country, and now the picture danced over the land, and Robinson thought he could see The Invention, his beloved machine, he thought he could actually see it smile, somehow, he was probably hallucinating now from the smoke, and he thought he could hear it speak, he could hear it say human words to him: "You wanted to see the future, here it is, and you're not in it, old man, thank your lucky stars." Robinson thought, God, my Invention, it's a bastard, a cruel bastard, it's playing with me, and he stood up to kick it, but there was too much smoke and he fell to the floor and the machine exploded and all the oil went up in flames.

Upon hearing an explosion, one of the neighbors ran down the stairs to see what was wrong, and saw smoke billowing out from the shelter door. He opened it, and letting in a great amount of oxygen at once, was subsumed by a great gulf of flame, which spread rather quickly into the President Shop, since the shop stood right there, on the ground floor, and the fire devoured everything—picture by picture, ornament by ornament, gulping its way through the wooden paneling, the aged curtains, until the windows started to burst under the pressure like firecrackers on a night of town festivities.

Chapter 51

THE FAMILY LEFT the National Restaurant and took a walk by the river. Diogen showed them his favorite tree, the honeyberry.

Ruben said, "These were brought over by the Austro-Hungarian colonizers, who had themselves brought them from Australia. Imagine that! A tree, traveling from so far away and making its home here."

The honeyberry had a trunk like taut muscles, a handsome tree with elongated leaves. Its spring buds peeked out. The family walked back onto the main street. Dusk was descending on the town.

Ruben said, "Let's go home, and rest."

He felt spent, wanted to, as Rosa had said, reorganize his energies for the season to come.

As they neared home, they saw two fire brigades, rotating lights on, and a big crowd of people. The firemen pointed large streams of water at the President Shop and out of that familiar space the fire danced wildly. The family paused.

Rosa said, "Is that the shop?"

Ruben said, "It can't be."

Mona and Diogen blinked against the light and the heat. They all stood suspended in a moment of mindlessness, disembodied almost. They watched as the flames engulfed the President Shop. Then, dropped back into the present moment, Ruben ran and Diogen hobbled over to the firemen, and Ruben could be heard shouting, "Oh my god, Oh my god!" and Diogen held Ruben back from running into the flames. Mona saw her father wave his fists at the fire and heard him shout "Put it out, put it out!"

The firemen carried Robinson out, entirely charred. All that remained of him were his thick glasses. In his hand was the projection lens that had been part of The Invention.

A fireman came out and said, "I don't know what to say, seems the old man had some kind of a machine down there that was soaked in so much petrol that it's a wonder the fire isn't worse. He had a dozen extra containers of petrol in there. The machine must have short-circuited and the whole place went up in flames. I've never seen anything like it."

Mona, who had remained stuck to the spot, still wearing her Youth Day outfit, watched the large five-pointed red star that adorned the shop's sign teased by the flames. The star was the size of an adult's torso and changed shades throughout the day, depending on the sunlight. Mona watched it melt and crackle in the heat. It was as if the flames were coming out to get a lick at it. The red plastic dripped, and then the star fell off its hinges, onto to the ground. Downstairs, The Invention had become a great mass of melted metal and plastic on the shelter floor. Robinson's sketches for The Truth Detector remained upstairs, hidden away inside his drawer. No one could make any sense of them.

Later, Ruben found the golden bust of the President, untouched inside its case. Nothing else was left of the President Shop.

Chapter 52

ROSA SITS AT the spring, atop the canyon. Mona is next to her. The sun is close to setting and they should make their way down soon. The day is warm. Ah how good life is, Rosa thinks, and what mystery envelops it. They can see a doe and a rabbit below, both nibbling on the greenery, and there are birds landing and taking off from the branches, and under the flutter of their wings the petals of a blossoming flower scatter down like snowflakes. A single bee works hard on a flower. It is filling its pockets with pollen, its tiny legs bulging with the golden powder. The river, at the bottom of the steep canyon, is swollen from the melted snow that pours in from the mountains. The world works, Rosa thinks, the world has order, regardless of human chaos. A butterfly lands on Mona's hand and she spreads out her fist so that it sits on her palm—it moves its wings open and shut slowly, they are sea blue, dotted with white like the shimmering sun atop the water's surface in midsummer. They watch the butterfly. At no moment does Mona move, her breath is quiet as she watches the creature, until it flies away. That's right, thinks Rosa. Don't grasp. Her heart is glad that her daughter chose to come up to the top with her; she strokes her hair and Mona puts her head in her mother's lap. Mona says, "Look, the swallows are back," and they watch the chattering flock rush past them overhead. The water from the spring flows evenly; it bites with freshness as it emerges from the heart of the mountain. The two women drink from it and wipe their lips with the back of their hands, and fill up their canisters.

"It's such good water," Rosa says, breathless from the drinking.

They had wild strawberries on the way up, searched for the tiny red heads hiding under their jagged leaves, and now they are ready to return home.

"Let's find some more strawberries on our way down," says Mona.

The forest takes them in and closes up behind them as they descend down the small mountain path.

About Sandorf Passage

SANDORF PASSAGE publishes work borne from displacement and movement that creates a prismatic perspective on what it means to live in a globalized world. It is a home to writing inspired by both conflict zones and the dangers of complacency. All Sandorf Passage titles share in common how the biggest and most important ideas are best explored in the most personal and intimate of spaces.